SPIDER SEASON

By BILLY HANSON

To
Rosie

10-5-18

Edited by ROZ WEISBERG
Illustrations by KARL SLOMINSKI

Printed in the United States of America
ISBN 978-1-54393-567-7 (print)
ISBN 978-1-54393-568-4 (ebook)

DIRIGO ENTERTAINMENT

SPIDER SEASON © 2018 by Dirigo Entertainment LLC
www.DirigoEntertainment.com

For my wife, who knows all of my stories before they're written.

THE STORIES

SPIDER SEASON

LIGHT SLEEPER

Trevor was having trouble sleeping. Over the last few weeks, he couldn't seem to get more than a few hours before waking at the sound of a rattling window or a raccoon scurrying across the roof. He and his wife Rebecca had recently moved into a new apartment near downtown LA, an old building that creaked and groaned with floors that screamed if you walked on the wrong spots. Somehow, their new landlord had convinced them that the hardwood was "most definitely worth" the extra hundred per month. It did look great, but at night it only made worse the troubles with Trevor's rest.

Wait, he thought with sudden alertness, *am I awake?* It was 3:33 in the morning. He didn't remember waking up.

He lay in bed, staring at the alarm clock, wide-eyed and breathing heavily. Despite the chill in the room, his skin was damp, hair matted to his forehead. For some reason, he was afraid, unable to piece together what had happened to him, like a drunk realizing that he's somehow made it home. He was sure the last thing he dreamt about was harmless. Something to do with playing football, which he rather hated, but it hadn't been a nightmare by any means. He hadn't been awake long, maybe less than 30 seconds, and his mind was starting to come back.

There had been a noise. A loud one. A bang, big enough to pull his body from sleep ahead of his wits.

"Not again, not tonight," he whispered to himself and rubbed his eyes. Rebecca stirred next to him but didn't wake. She never woke up at night. Not like he did.

He was tired enough to cry and awake enough to realize he wouldn't get back to sleep easily. If he had to spend another morning chugging cups of disgusting office coffee, another afternoon nodding off during a meeting, or another evening sinking deeper and deeper into the couch, he would be willing to up and move right then. He couldn't keep waking up every night. It had to stop.

Trevor's scrawny arms shivered, his bones rattled in his elbows. They had left the fan on last night, only for the white noise. Total silence in their new, cavernous apartment

2

would have kept Trevor awake, allowing his mind to spin into an unwitting overdrive. So, he always left the fan humming on low at the foot of the bed, pointed at the bottom of his feet. There was a constant blast of cold air from his toes to his chin. Rebecca had wrapped herself up in the blankets like a burrito, leaving him with enough of the comforter to cover only about a third of his left leg. If only to avoid frostbite, Trevor willed his body into motion and reclaimed his half of the blankets.

As warmth spread through his body again, he rolled from his right side to his left, then back again. His pillow suddenly felt too thin and there was a twinge in his neck that tightened more every second. *What was that bang? Did something fall over, or maybe come loose from the wall and drop to the floor?* The only problem with that explanation is that nothing followed. Nothing spilled or rolled, no glass shattered. Just a single heavy THWAP! It sounded, Trevor thought, like an open hand smacking the wall down the hallway. But what sense did that make? Eyes glued to the obnoxiously bright alarm clock, Trevor allowed a wry smile at the silly thought.

With nothing to do but fidget nervously and wonder what the sound could have been, he rolled onto his back to stare up at the ceiling. Stretching wouldn't loosen the new knot at the base of his neck. Even with the cold on his skin dissipating, his goose bumps remained, and his body was still on high-alert, still tensed up.

Something was wrong. That sound. No, not a sound, it was a definite BANG and it came from just outside his bedroom door. Trevor wasn't one to let his imagination run away with itself, but now his mind whirred with possibilities. His panic set in. His heavy breathing wouldn't slow. *What the fuck WAS that?*

Clang! Trevor jumped at the clashing of metal against metal as the dog shifted in his crate. Oscar shook his head, then his butt, making himself comfortable, like he hadn't scared the shit out of anyone.

"Oscar, no!" Trevor grumbled, more a reaction than a command.

The Wheaten Terrier picked his head up from the soft cushion in his crate and stared at him dazed and sleepy, irritated. Once Oscar realized that he wouldn't be scolded any further, he snorted and put his head back down. Rebecca was still dead asleep on her side of the bed. She hadn't heard the bang or the dog; Trevor was jealous of her ability to simply turn to stone when she fell asleep. It was a trait that Trevor had admired at first, but now it annoyed him every time he lay awake at 4am and she shook the windows with vicious snoring.

Years ago, in their old Hollywood neighborhood, a

series of gunshots ripped through the night from down the block. Trevor came dangerously close to wetting the bed. Rebecca never stirred. Their walls were thin, so the shots might as well have been right outside the window. The whole neighborhood buzzed with excitement and fear for hours. Trevor had to tell Rebecca about it the next morning, speaking at length about the circling helicopters and police lights filling their room with flashing red and blue. How she slept through that, he'd never know.

The clock ticked over to 3:46AM. Trevor was wide awake and no less petrified. It didn't seem like he and his wife were in any immediate danger, but that bang echoed in his head, refusing to move to the back of his mind. He rubbed his eyes again in frustration, but he was too scared to put his arms outside of the blanket for long, so he yanked them right back under. His feet were pulled up in the fetal position, shoving his back against Rebecca's arm. He felt like he was five years old, sleeping alone in a strange new room that he didn't like.

This is ridiculous, he thought. With a quick inhale to gather his courage, he stretched out his legs and pulled his arms out from under the blanket. His muscles loosened and his bones creaked almost as loud as the floor. He already felt better. Now he had to go out and look. He had to know what that noise was. There was no way he'd be able to sleep again without at least some idea of what happened out there, and he'd had too many sleepless nights lately.

Even though his own mind warned him against keeping his arms outside of the shield of his blanket, Trevor held both arms out in defiance, stretching the rest of the sleep from his limbs.

See? Nothing, he thought proudly, trying to convince himself that he wasn't scared. He had been afraid of the dark a long time ago, the way that all children are, but now that he was an adult, the dark was always welcome after a long and stressful da–

BANG!

Trevor's arms shot back under the blanket, fast enough to throw an elbow into Rebecca's right arm, but she barely stirred. He'd have to explain that bruise in the morning, but there was the sound again. That same massive BANG! Now hearing it while fully conscious, Trevor knew it was in the hallway, much closer to their room than he liked and that lingering cold in his spine moved like an icy wind through his guts. He cowered in the bed, back under the protection of his comforter.

But Trevor wasn't going to lay in bed and simply wait to be murdered. He gathered all the courage he could, slid the blanket off his body and lowered his feet down to the floor, as quietly as possible. If there was something out there, he didn't want it to know that he was awake. Trevor wasn't a big guy. He was tall, but lanky. A runner, not a fighter. But he was scrappy, and with the element of surprise on his side, he thought could win a fight with an intruder.

The hardwood floors were somehow even colder than his feet. The bed creaked as he shifted his weight from the mattress to the floor. Trevor eyed the door, focused on the glass knob, half expecting it to turn. But it didn't move. Not yet, anyway. When he put all his weight on his feet, the floorboards betrayed him. They rubbed together so loudly he thought he might have broken one. He stopped and waited to see if there would be a response from outside his door. *Maybe*, he thought, *the floorboards in the hallway will be on my side and give me a sign that something is out there.* He listened but heard nothing. Somehow that was worse.

With his cover blown, Trevor crept across the bedroom toward the dresser. He stepped on dirty laundry, pushed around the boxes of books they had yet to unpack, and did his best to avoid the loudest parts of the floor. The top drawer of his dresser slid open and he reached into the pile of folded socks. He rooted around shoving aside a belt, a watch, for a moment worried that what he was looking for was not actually there, that he'd left it packed in some random bag and would never be able to find it before his door burst open with a blood-sucking vampire ready to drain them both. But that's when his fingers grazed the small box and he lifted it out with momentary relief.

The knife inside was a gift from his wife's uncle. Receiving a lethal weapon for Christmas in front of his in-laws struck him as lunacy, but Trevor had thanked him politely and pretended to check the blade's sharpness, as if he knew what he was doing. He never would have bought a knife for himself, even after living in LA for nearly a decade. He doubted he'd be able to actually stab somebody, should the situation arise, but if there really was an intruder, he would have to thank Uncle Robbie profusely the next time he saw him.

Trevor flipped the blade up and made sure it was locked into place before turning back toward the door. He took a step forward and waded carefully through the mess of clothes, but his toes caught on something. He kicked his foot out of the tangle of jeans or whatever the hell Rebecca had left by his side of the bed and accidentally yanked the fan cord right out of the wall. The blades quickly slowed and came to a stop, leaving the room in complete, devastating silence.

Trevor held his breath. He moved even slower than before. The heavy quiet made every breath a scream, every footstep an earthquake. The silence also revealed a rustling sound on the other side of the door, but it was hard to tell what exactly it was. It sounded like only the wind against the walls, but in his heightened state, any sound at all would put him on edge.

A memory crept up then, one that seemed funny before, but now made him feel stupid for not seeing it as a warning. On a lazy Sunday evening the week before, Oscar had been playing fetch up and down the hallway, his favorite game, when he stopped on a dime and glared at nothing behind Rebecca. She and Trevor giggled like idiots until Oscar started whimpering. Something in the shadows had scared him. They assumed it was a spider. It was the season for them after all. They couldn't go two days without finding one in the shower or the laundry. But they didn't find one that day. Maybe Oscar saw something they hadn't. He wondered if that thing was on the other side of the door now.

Trevor shook the odd memory out of his head and continued toward the door, knife in hand, ready to strike. He flipped the knife and pointed the blade up; he'd heard you have more control of the blade that way. Where had he heard that? Probably a TV show and it was probably wrong. He looked down at the shiny metal, his eyes adjusted to the darkness, and swiped the air with a few quick jabs to test out his agility with a blade.

Shit, he thought, *knife's not gonna do much good if it's a ghost.*

As he reached for the doorknob, he prayed he would

only find darkness beyond it. He didn't know if he'd be able to kill anyone, but with his wife asleep in the bedroom, he knew he had to try. His hand wrapped around the glass knob and as quietly as he could, he twisted it. It made a loud cracking sound, shifting inside the old wood of the door. If something was out there, it knew he was coming out.

Trevor pushed open the door and peered into the long, dark hallway. Weak yellow light spilled in through the curtains from the side window. Ten feet in front of him, the whole apartment fell into full darkness. Trevor's plea for an empty hallway was granted, but as with most wishes, it turned out to be the opposite of what he truly wanted.

What the hell made that sound? He thought about calling out into the dark, but the air caught in his throat.

The light switch was near the office, halfway down the hall, well into the darkness. Trevor crept forward, realizing how cold the place was. Their building was built in the 1920s, so everything was wide open and drafty, which was fantastic during hot summer days when the breeze was a lifesaver, but now, just before winter, the cold stuck to the walls, swirled around the rooms, down the hallway and through his bones.

The creaky floors squealed again as Trevor stepped into the black. The knife was still clutched in his fist, ready to stab at anything that leapt from the shadows. His other hand reached out for the switch, but Trevor pulled it back when he realized that he would have to reach across the open door of the office to flip it on. The killer could easily be lurking in the pitch-black room, waiting for him to reach out across the opening where he or she could swing a machete down on his arm, cutting it off at the elbow. There's no way he was reaching out for the light now, not with that image in his head. Instead, He put his back to the opposite wall and slid over to peek into the office from as far back as he could get. Nervously, he stepped past the door and looked straight into the empty room, nobody was there.

In that moment of opportunity, Trevor lunged forward and flipped the light switch up, an action Rebecca would have called cartoonish and silly, had she been awake to see it. Bright light flooded the hallway, revealing the empty office and part of the kitchen. With nothing in front of him to cut, he lowered the knife and finally exhaled. He walked into the office and turned on that light too, for good measure. Nothing. His laptop was there, as was his iPad. A burglar would have seen those and snatched them, for sure. He left the light on and walked down the hallway toward the kitchen, a confident new bounce in his step.

The floor lamp switched on with a pop, its brand new LED bulbs buzzed and the place lit up like it was daytime. Trevor looked around the cupboards for a moment, sure he would find a plate or a mug that had fallen and shattered. They were still unpacking the kitchen after all, so things may have shifted around, or a box crumpled under the weight of whatever was piled on top of it. But he found nothing out of place. Everything remained where they'd left it the night before. He switched off the light, the fear completely drained from his body now. His arms and legs felt loose and free, the muscles in his neck finally let go of their tense grip.

After a quick once-over in the dining room and living room, Trevor felt a million times better, if a bit childish for being so scared in the first place. The front door was still locked and dead-bolted, the windows all closed and secured, the TV off. Trevor thought for a moment about watching a movie since he was up, but with his fear subsided and the adrenaline slowing, his eyes grew heavy again.

"Damn, I need to get some sleep," he mumbled to himself and grabbed a granola bar as he walked through the kitchen. He knew damn well that eating before sleeping gave you bad dreams, but he was starved and at 4am with only a couple hours left to sleep, he could handle a nightmare.

As he worked through the loud wrapper of the granola bar, his mind drifted back to the bang. *What had that been, anyway?* With a grin pasted on one corner of his mouth, he decided it didn't matter. There was nothing in the house and nothing was broken. He and Rebecca loved their new place, loved how big and open and old fashioned it was. If it came with a few quirks and some new noises for them to adjust to, so be it. It was an old building, what did they expect?

He moved back down the hallway and turned off all the lights that he'd turned on. The place fell into darkness again. Trevor finished the bar in two huge bites, and with a mouthful of nuts and raisins, tossed the wrapper into the office trashcan. With no more regard for the creaking floorboards, he walked back to the bedroom door and twisted the knob. Rebecca was of course asleep, mouth agape, snoring ever so lady-like.

BANG!

Trevor whipped around, the sound only a few feet behind him. It sounded like a baseball bat hitting a thin plank of wood. His relief at finding nothing in the light now felt like a momentary break from reality. Trevor reached into the pocket of his pajama bottoms, but he'd left the knife on the kitchen counter. With Rebecca still dead to the world in the bed, he raced toward the hallway light switch. This time in a frenzy, he reached across the open office door.

The moment before his fingers touched the switch, a hulking, silhouetted figure leapt out of the empty room, grabbed his arm and let loose a high-pitched squeal.

An arm draped in thick black cloth shoved Trevor

away from the switch and forced his body to the ground. His cheek hit the floor with a distinct crunch. He tried to yell, but a second hand covered his mouth. His free arm flailed, grasped at the air behind him, his eyes searched wildly for any sign of who or what was attacking him.

Oh god, it's real, his mind screamed. The figure wore a deep hood that shielded its face. It let out a growl like an animal about to sink its teeth into a nice meal. Trevor tried again to twist his back to get a look behind him, but the thing had him pinned.

"Who are you?" he pleaded.

The thing answered with a deep throated clicking. Then it plunged something into Trevor's lower back, cutting through the dense muscle, scraping against his spine. The tip of the knife hit the hardwood floor and finally stopped.

He couldn't scream through the creature's hand, but he opened his mouth wide in shock. The chill of fear that had spread from his neck was replaced with hot, searing pain as the figure pulled the knife from his back with a sickening rip.

The blood pooled on the wood around him, staining the expensive floor.

The dark figure reached down and grabbed Trevor's hair, pulling his head up and back, exposing his throat. In his final moments, Trevor wanted to know what it was, where it came from, how it made that banging sound without being seen.

But he only muttered a single, blood-soaked word, "Why?"

The thing leaned down, its head dipped into the yellow light of the street lamp. Trevor saw its face. It looked human, only not quite assembled properly.

"Because you came looking," it hissed into his ear.

Trevor caught a glimpse of the strange, curved blade in the figure's hand. No, not a hand, some sort of claw, scaly and greenish gray. Trevor wanted to scream all over again.

What the fuck is–, Trevor's final thought was cut short as the long blade raked across his throat and sliced through his windpipe and arteries with ease. More blood shot onto the floor in quick, gushing bursts. His head dropped and his eyes fell to the bedroom door, still cracked open.

Finished with its work on Trevor, the murderous figure stood and turned its attention to the bedroom door–to Rebecca, sound asleep and happily dreaming.

With his last breath, Trevor watched the figure raise a hand and pound on the wall outside the door. One hit, a single loud bang that rattled the windows and shook the cupboards. Trevor smiled to himself.

Good luck, he thought, *she'll sleep through the end of the world.*

He rested his head gently on the floor, in the pool of his own thickening blood. He grew more tired by the second.

At last, Trevor closed his eyes and drifted off to sleep.

THE CLEARING

AUGUST 7th, 1976

Northern Maine felt hotter in that afternoon than any other day that summer, though the news said it was only in the low 70s. Jeremy Lawson wiped his brow, leaving his glove dripping with sweat, though his skin replaced the moisture within seconds. He loathed the unrelenting sun, his hatred only serving to intensify his body heat. His skin was sticky, his eyes stung with sweat, his clothes hung too thick and baggy. His muscles ached after three hours of hacking away at the same tree trunk. His efforts had little effect on the dense wood. The work, mind-numbing and repetitive, destroyed more of his willpower with every chop of the ax.

A month ago, Jeremy made his own decision to come back to the lumber yard. He didn't even get to enjoy the righteous anger that men feel when they've been forced into a bad situation. He'd chosen to wake up at 4am every morning, drive for 90 minutes into the deep woods to swing an ax for 10 straight hours, all while swatting away a constant swarm of mosquitoes, his skin baking in the sun. His job options were limited, so the choice to return to the woods now felt like a punishment.

Most days, the ax allowed him to work out the usual frustrations. He could imagine he was knocking some sense into his boss, occasionally his wife. But today was different. A twisted feeling of anger brewed in his stomach, slowly hardening into hatred. Of what, he wasn't sure, but every swing made his face hotter, his throat drier. It felt less like he was chopping wood and more like he was carving his own path into hell. He could have sworn he smelled sulfur out there in the middle of the woods.

"Fuck this," Jeremy muttered to himself and slammed his ax into the trunk once more, leaving it stuck there. He picked up his bottle and took a swig of hot water (*of course it's fucking hot*). He stood for a moment, a tall, bulky statue of a man and watched the other guys work, all happily chop, chop, chopping away at the trees. *Lemmings, the lot of them.* The sound of the work, that steady, damp thud of axes against the trees could be oddly calming, until it was broken by the sudden, loud crack of the splitting wood. They'd cleared a shocking amount of land in just a couple weeks. They were doing good work. But now there was no shade. The sun beat down on them all, roasting them in a fire pit that they themselves were building.

These other guys somehow thrived in this job, happy to work with their hands, the obvious and tangible progress must have been fulfilling. Jeremy couldn't give two shits about working with his hands. He'd work in an office if he could. He would answer phones, take meeting notes, deliver mail, whatever was needed. But he couldn't type and wasn't the best communicator, so here he was. The great outdoors. He'd put "Outdoor Work" as the absolute last option on the form he'd filled out at the placement office.

The employment counselor read his application, looked him over and said, "You've got arms, you can chop trees." She hadn't said that exactly, but Jeremy knew what she meant.

He'd put up with this kind of summer for three goddamn years. Aroostook County didn't have much work that wasn't on a lumber yard or a potato farm. Jeremy had lived in Madawaska for his entire life, born and raised around farms, trees, and tree farms. He was no stranger to hard work. At 36, he still hated these summer jobs, but he'd always found a way to suck it up, get through them. He was surprised that he felt so rotten about it now. There was something about that day, the air around the whole place, the empty space in the dense forest that they'd taken down against the will of Mother Nature. Something was wrong with the clearing.

Jeremy stomped toward the makeshift base camp – *that's what they call the two fucking coolers and rickety old shack* – leaving his ax lodged in the stump behind him. As he walked, he saw the land manager, Mark, watching from a distance, but Jeremy would take the scolding. He couldn't swing that ax again, at least not for a few minutes. A write-up from a little weasel like Mark wouldn't phase him. He tore down the hill, the heat and humidity stoking his disdain for the Aroostook Lumber Company and for his small part in it. He was worried that he would boil over if he couldn't cool down soon.

As he approached base camp, the expression he saw on Mark's face became clear. He was scared. Jeremy couldn't blame him, though. There had been a scary incident with a man a few weeks back, old John Cloninger from Lisbon. Not used to the physical labor that came with the title of lumberjack, John had gotten upset and dove head-first into a screaming match with Mark and another supervisor, threatening to sue them over the work conditions, even though every other man was dealing with the heat. John

Cloninger had nearly killed a man that day when he threw his ax in anger, sending it flipping end over end through the clearing. It had narrowly missed one of the other workers, who had to take the next day off because of the shock of nearly losing his head.

Jeremy hadn't reached that point yet. He thought he could snap at someone, end up in an argument with Mark over the working conditions, but he wouldn't be throwing any axes. He doubted he could muster the strength to raise his voice. Although when he saw Mark approaching with his wobbly, unbalanced march, he already felt that pissed off energy collecting in his gut.

Jeremy's eyes stung. He rubbed his face, knowing it wouldn't help. But he felt the unrelenting urge to do something, anything to distract himself from the dirty feel of his skin. It was torturous. He went home every day feeling like he'd been stretched, pulled and spread out over the muddy ground. His life had become a useless routine; wake up before sunrise, ride with a bunch of hillbillies to the deep woods, chop down trees until after sunset, get home, take a shower, sit on the couch watch late night TV for about twenty minutes, then go to sleep to start the whole mess over again. He was miserably tired, well beyond what a good night's sleep or a day off could fix.

He stepped into the tent and found the cooler that held the drinks. Surely, the ice would all be melted by now, but even slightly cooler water would be refreshing. He needed to calm himself down. Getting himself worked up was only going to make everything worse, make his skin stickier and bring more bugs to crawl around on it. He slapped more bugs from his neck, starting to think that mosquitoes were attracted to the anger. The cooler flipped up and he pulled one of the full water bottles from the bottom. The ice was long gone, but the water was cool enough.

Jeremy sighed loudly as he unscrewed the bottle and poured the water onto his head and face. It was glorious relief for a few quick seconds. For a moment, he thought he'd be able to pull himself together and finish out the day. But that bliss was short lived. As the initial shock of cool water passed, his skin heated up again, his face feeling even hotter than before. He poured more on himself, draining the bottle. Again, the momentary relief was squashed when his sunburned cheeks all but turned the water to steam.

He felt a sudden panic in his chest, and he pulled at the buttons of his shirt. He wanted to rip off all his clothes, lay in the dirt, pour the cooler water over himself and roll around in the mud. But before he'd gotten three buttons loose, Mark walked into the tiny shack.

"Is there a problem, Mr. Lawson?"

Jeremy paused for a moment. He should have expected an audience.

"It's too goddamn hot out there," he mumbled, wanting to say more.

"Well, we've got more waters on the way."

"No, it's..." Jeremy felt something rising in him, an inner cold front, frosting everything from his gut to his throat. He bit his tongue, able to stifle whatever it was that was trying to force its way out. "It's not just the heat. I can't think out there, I can barely breathe. My skin is crawling with fucking mosquitoes, man."

"There's bug spray in the trunk, Jer-"

"I don't need the fucking bug spray, Mark. I need to get out of here before I lose my goddamn mind." His anger turned desperate. "Give me a truck."

Mark was taken aback.

"You can't take a truck."

"I can't stay here."

"Jeremy, you're not taking a truck. If there's an emergency, we won't have a way out."

"This is an emergency, you little shit." His fingers clenched into trembling fists.

"Mr. Lawson, you signed a contract which guarantees that you work in this forest for the full week. Now if you want out of that contract, we can discuss it back at the office this evening, but under no circumstances will I put these other men at risk because you don't like the flies." Mark added a comical little nod to further punctuate his sentence.

A moment of quiet hung in the air. Jeremy realized that he was biting his tongue. The taste of iron filled his mouth, and the sharp pain brought a moment's clarity. It wasn't Mark who was making the sun burn or the bugs bite. He was a weasel, but he was doing his job. He didn't look any happier than the rest of them. Jeremy softened, forcing himself to calm down.

"Okay, I'm sorry. I'm... It's too goddamn hot out here."

Mark popped open the cooler and pulled out another bottle of water, handing it over. "Then let's head up the hill and get back to work, shall we? Got a lot of trees to drop today."

Mark motioned to the door. Jeremy was coming down from the anger, breaking through to the other side of his rage and heading toward the familiar complacency. He followed Mark out into the clearing. They marched up the hill, the heat intensifying as they left the shade. As they walked, Jeremy saw the back of Mark's shirt. It was completely dry. There was no sweat on his back, under his arms, on his collar, nowhere. They reached Jeremy's tree, where his ax remained stuck in the trunk and faced each other.

"You think you can get back to chopping now, and quit the whining?" If he'd just left off the whining comment, it could have ended there.

Something awoke in Jeremy that he never realized was there. It had lain dormant his whole life, waiting for this moment, this exact confluence of weather, people, words and mental state, and now it tore out of his mind and through his body, seizing control of his limbs. Jeremy lunged. He grabbed Mark's neck and shoved his face down onto the nearby stump. Mark's head hit the wood with a sickening snap as his cheekbone splintered, and he was sent into a daze.

"You want me to chop?!" Jeremy yanked his ax head from the stump. A couple other lumberjacks turned at the sound of screaming. Jeremy raised the ax swing up as high as he could get it, then with a grunt of effort, he brought it down onto the side of Mark's face. The crunch was quick; the sound wet. Mark's face came clean off his head in one piece. It slid over the side of the stump, plopping onto the ground with a damp smack. His body shuddered for a moment before going limp and dropping into the dirt, blood oozing from the massive wound.

"I kept my ax good and sharp for ya, pal! Just like the handbook said!" he screamed at the corpse. The heat didn't matter to him now. Everything was red, the cut down trees, the grass, the people. The clearing had gotten a hold of him. There was nothing he could do, he had already crossed the line and a man lay dead. He didn't care. It was too fucking hot.

It was dead quiet in the clearing. Jeremy looked around at the men in front of him, all of them wide-eyed with shock and disbelief. All the work stopped. A few seconds went by before anyone moved.

As the first man charged him, Jeremy allowed the fury to continue. He raised the ax high, stepped to his left and swung just as his attacker lunged for him. The blade jammed into the dense muscle of the man's neck. He fell, dead before he hit the dirt. Jeremy ripped the ax free and turned to the others. His eyes were terribly bloodshot, his face stretched tight in rage, his veins ready to burst out of his skin, and Jeremy shouted with a distorted, inhuman voice.

"Come on, everybody! Let's find some fucking shade!"

***

JANUARY 14th, 2018

Henry's attraction to Gabby was magnetic. Whatever she was about, he was 100% in. He stared at her, only half-aware he was doing so, admiring her tight grey sweater and high-waisted jeans from across the classroom. It wasn't a particularly revealing outfit, but she looked good. She could have worn a potato sack and his eyes would still be glued to her. She'd effortlessly won him over when she played Ophelia the previous semester, and now their assigned seats in Geometry were scandalously close to each other, so there was no escape for him. It all seemed pretty normal for an awkward, wiry sixteen-year-old guy.

The bell rang and Henry was jolted out of his day dream. *Dammit,* he thought, angry with himself, *this is my one class with Gabby today and I wasted it daydreaming about her. I could have done that from home.*

To Henry, Gabby was all-consuming. He gazed at her all day and at night, his dreams were flooded with a sea of wavy black hair and startlingly bright green eyes that froze him solid like she was an angelic Medusa. To say that she was his crush would be an absurd understatement. She was his cosmic match. Their pairing was a universal truth, an inevitability that would occur naturally if only they weren't shackled by the world, society, and the infamous love killer, high school.

He watched her routinely pack up her books, laugh with her friends, and walk out of the classroom, beyond his reach for another weekend. He let out a heavy sigh and grabbed his things to start the trek home.

The hallway was jam-packed. Students shoved their way through the crowd, excited about the two days off. Henry was always a bit confused about the thrill of a Friday, especially during the coldest time of year. People like Gabby might head up to Sunday River to go skiing, but this far into the season, even that was probably getting old. For the kids whose families couldn't afford weekend ski trips, it would be a day at the movies or basement hangouts until dinner time. One way or another, they all did what Henry did; got together with friends and annoyed their parents with obnoxious entertainment. That was winter in Maine.

Henry kept his head down and his bag tight against his back. His friend Tommy would no doubt be looking for him by the gym so they could plan their entire weekend down to the minute, but he didn't have enough energy to deal with Tommy just yet. Maybe after a Mountain Dew and a candy bar on the walk home he'd shoot Tommy a text to see what he wanted to do. But for now, he'd probably just head home, unwind, watch a bit of porn, and relax.

The thought of porn brought Gabby to his mind again. In his head, that grey sweater of hers ripped off with ease, her high waisted jeans slid down her smooth dark legs with no resistance and his hands were there to caress every inch of skin she revealed to him. He felt a bit guilty equating her with the raunchy (arguably filthy) images he jerked off to, but that's how his mind worked. He wanted to fuck her, plain and simple. So did all the other guys. But he liked her. He wanted all that dirty stuff, but he also wanted to be the guy to make her laugh all day, the guy she ran up to in the hallway and planted a big sloppy kiss on.

Frigid January air and blinding white snow greeted Henry as he walked out of the building. He threw on his sunglasses and kept pushing forward through the riotous "bus kids", always shouting and cackling while in line. He avoided the obnoxious group and moved toward the street, on his usual path home. The bus kids were falling out of earshot when another grating voice broke into his calm.

"Henry! Hey man, slow up." Tommy McKenna spotted him and jogged down the sidewalk to catch up. Henry sighed, which he couldn't hide in the cold air, but Tommy didn't seem to notice or care.

"Hey Tommy," he grumbled.

"Where you off to man? I thought we were hangin' out."

"I know," Henry didn't hide his annoyance, "but I want to head home first, lay down for a while."

"Dude, if you need whack time, I understand." Tommy waited for a laugh, like no one knew he was going to make that joke. Henry wasn't usually so annoyed with vulgar jokes, but he actually had been considering a little "whack time", so he was more defensive than he usually would be. Henry sighed loudly again. This time Tommy noticed.

"Okay, call me after you clean up and we'll play some Call of Duty or something."

He waited a couple seconds for Henry's response, but when he saw that he wouldn't get a chuckle or even a grin to play along, he rolled his eyes, turned around, and moved toward the parking lot.

"Or just text me when you get your fucking beauty sleep, man," Tommy shot back.

Henry kept walking, putting in earbuds to drown out everything and everyone. Tommy had gotten the message, maybe a little clearer than Henry meant to send it, but at least he was on his own again. He'd have to apologize later, but his only goal that afternoon was to be in his own head for a while.

About halfway home, Henry was alone on the sidewalk. Now that he was a good distance from the school, foot traffic was almost non-existent. He passed the occasional old man walking his dog, or a mailman miserable in the cold, but he walked right past, ignoring them all. He'd about gotten himself back to normal when a voice from behind made him jump.

"Henry!" It was a girl's voice, a familiar one. His head

whipped around, eyes wide in shock. He immediately wished he had reacted any other way when he found Gabby there with a wide smile, proud of her sneak attack. Henry let loose a forced smile to hide his inner terror, trying to act cool about it. The last thing he wanted to be was a wimp.

"Shit, you scared me," he said with a laugh.

"I know, sorry. I saw the opportunity and I couldn't resist." Her voice was light and soothing. If it hadn't been so cold outside, Henry might have melted then and there.

"I tried to convince her to shove you into the snow," Rob Kipling stepped forward with a less genuine smile. Henry hadn't seen him standing behind Gabby. Adoration and loathing began the fight for Henry's attention. He and Rob had never liked each other, not even when they were five years old and had no grudges to hold. Every time they found themselves in a room together, one of them would find a reason to leave, or at least move to the opposite wall.

When he'd first heard about Gabby and Rob dating, Henry was flummoxed. This was the goddess of the 11th grade accepting as her partner the moron who'd flunked his sophomore gym class. But his explanation was the same as every other loser whose crush likes someone else. Rob was better than him. His family had money, he played basketball, always hung out with the popular crowd. People insisted he was funny, but he'd never made Henry laugh.

Henry managed, "Well as long as there's no yellow snow around, that's cool." Gabby favored him with a pity chuckle. Rob put his arm around her shoulders.

"Come on babe, we should keep walking," Rob said, already finished with the conversation. It was a deep cut into Henry's heart to see Gabby walking around with this asshole. His hair was comically gelled into a faux-hawk. Huge, expensive sunglasses, too flashy for a high school kid, sat propped on his nose. One of Rob's favorite hobbies was driving his Dodge Challenger around the school parking lot, showing it off to other students that he assumed were impressed. Somehow, none of that deterred Gabby, because there she was, perfectly content at his side.

"I thought you had a car, Gabby. Just felt like a midday stroll?" Henry reminded himself to smile.

"Rob's taking me out to that spot in the woods," Gabby said, "that clearing that's supposed to be haunted."

"It's not haunted, it's got a curse on it," Rob said.

"Oh, the Lawson Clearing. Yeah, I heard about it. I don't know about curses, but I hear it's pretty cool." Henry said with confidence.

"Seriously bro, it's got a curse on it. It's either ancient Native burial grounds or like guardian spirits or something, but shit's crazy. Like five different people have lost their minds after spending too much time there." Rob's face lit up.

He was excited to go.

Gabby chimed in, "I read that in 1974, there was a logger who went nuts and hacked 5 people to death with an axe before they were able to restrain him. Then in the 80s, some woman got obsessed with the place, so she kept taking her kids camping out there. Then, they went missing and cops found the two kids tied up and shot, and the mother starved to death looking over their bodies."

"You seem far too giddy about those stories," Henry joked.

Gabby hid a shy smile, embarrassed that her nerdy excitement was showing. Henry guessed that she could have spoken about the clearing's macabre history for hours. But Rob jumped in and ruined their chemistry. Of course.

"I went up there last summer with a couple guys from the team and it got real weird, real fast. You know Parker Morris, the quiet kid in our class? He got out there and started a fight with Guy Ashcraft. Got the piss beat out of him, but I've never seen that kid make a peep hanging out with us. Two minutes in the clearing and he thinks he's Muhammed Ali. They say that place brings out your baser instincts whether you want them out or not. That's why we're going out there, anyway." Rob came up behind Gabby and mimed humping her. She didn't find that funny.

"Rob, knock it off. That's gross." Gabby pulled away

from him.

"We'll see how gross you think it is when we get there," his knowing smile was awful.

"Henry, you want to come with us, check it out?" Henry knew the invite was punishment for Rob being so crass, not a real invitation, but part of him wanted to say yes and latch himself onto their romantic outing. But he couldn't find a way to go without sounding pathetic and desperate.

"Nah, I should get home. I told Tommy I'd play some Xbox with him, and believe me, if I'm not online in like 30 minutes, I'll start getting angry phone calls until I log in." Gabby laughed at that, a full, whole-hearted, honest-to-god laugh. That alone turned Henry's day around.

"Okay, rain check then. We'd better go before we freeze to death on the sidewalk." She gave a cute little bounce and added, "See ya!"

Rob threw his arm around her again and they walked by Henry, moving toward the woods. He watched as they pushed through the deep snow near the tree line. Rob turned around then, having thought of something else worth yelling out to him.

"Couldn't talk her into any dirty stuff at home, so hopefully her animal instincts have more to offer in the woods!"

Henry's heart pounded. Gabby smacked him playfully

in the head, then immediately curled under his arm and continued through the dense trees.

Henry had always hated Rob, but never more than in that moment. Now he had Gabby in his arms, talking about fucking her in the woods. Henry clenched his fists and squeezed his eyes as tight as he could, containing his righteous anger.

Henry turned toward home. He was livid. The thought of Gabby naked with Rob enraged him even further; rolling around in the snow, faces contorted with pleasure, his shoulders flexing as he pumped and thrusted, her back arched in a climax so intense that she couldn't help but scream. Within a few seconds, his mind was racing, searching for a way to stop it from happening. He pulled on his shaggy hair and growled, keeping himself from screaming.

When he finally took a step from the sidewalk, it wasn't toward home. He marched toward the tree line, toward Rob and Gabby, toward Lawson's Clearing. If Henry confronted Rob in the woods, it would lead to a fight. Rob would beat him senseless. But it wouldn't matter. Gabby obviously didn't want to have sex with Rob, she'd said it plainly, but Rob was still going to try. Who would Henry be if he let horrible people hurt his friends like that?

He walked on top of their footprints, stomping and muttering to himself the whole way, getting himself ready for a fight.

★★★

After what felt like an hour of walking, Gabby stepped into the clearing with an unexpected sense of awe. It was massive, much bigger than she'd thought it was going to be. She was sure they could see for miles, but really it wasn't more than a few acres in any direction. It was insane that people had come in and cleared an area this big, only to abandon the project. It was breathtaking with the coat of smooth, white snow. The sheet was only broken by a few tall stumps and a smattering of animal tracks. The wind swirled around the clearing in circles, sending a handful of loose leaves and twigs tumbling through the open field, the constant breeze blowing her hair into her face. She smelled the fresh air, crisp and cold and realized she'd never been anywhere so untainted by the world. Her eyes watered against the chilly air. She was overwhelmed by the enormity of the place.

She turned back to Rob, who had stopped to piss in the bushes behind her and asked, "How could this place be haunted?"

"Cursed," he corrected, zipping up his pants. He stepped up behind Gabby and wrapped her up the way she liked, arms around her midsection, below her breasts, his chin resting on her shoulder. Her body warmed as she nestled into him.

"Fine, cursed."

Rob placed a tiny kiss her neck. A light, unassuming kiss. It sent a shiver down her spine. Rob felt her seize for a second, and he planted a kiss on the other side of her neck, this one assuming a lot. Gabby brushed him off and stepped away, into the clearing. The breeze pulled her softly toward its center, where the snow was completely smooth like white glass. Her hair stood on end as she moved away from the trees. A hollow pit in her stomach grew more and more the further into the clearing she went. Despite her company, she felt alone, vulnerable.

There was a small broken-down shack to her right with an old sign for the Aroostook Lumber Company on the ground next to it. It had fallen off decades earlier and suffered the seasons in the dirt. Gabby stopped walking near the center of the clearing. The shack unlocked an old memory. She'd read about that shack, seen pictures of it when the sign was still up. A cold front seized her chest, stopping her breath.

"That's where the axe guy killed everyone." Rob said. He wasn't making any progress getting her clothes off, so he could indulge in the macabre of the place. Gabby locked her eyes on the hill and stared in wide-eyed disbelief.

"I recognize it."

"Yeah, he was this guy just having a rough day,

decided to chop his buddies to pieces. Then after that mom killed her kids out here, people started avoiding this place. Crazy."

"They all died right here," Gabby said. She looked around her. She was standing in the center, where the family had perished. Her shoulders shook as another chill rattled her spine.

Gabby couldn't help but be impressed with the place. Hauntings were bullshit. Based on everything she'd read, the stories about Lawson's Clearing were nothing more than people letting their imaginations run wild. But standing there, in the center of the enchanting field, knowing that people had suffered horrible things, her imagination geared up for a wild run of its own.

"Holy shit," she muttered to herself, the weight of the clearing overwhelming her.

Rob smiled and put his arm around her. "You feel anything different?"

Gabby did feel different, but not in the way he meant. She was awe-struck.

Under her breath, she said, "I had no idea it would be like this. It's amazing."

Rob perked up when he saw her eyes brighten. Maybe she'd be open to messing around after all. He'd only half thought he could convince her of the place's romantic power. He didn't need to start his bullshit spiel about the beauty of the sun on the ice, or the quiet stillness and serenity. She saw that already. He'd still have to convince her that the clearing was completely private, but he could do that.

"Feel like you're losing your inhibitions, yet?"

"Maybe a little," she said, meaning to sound inspired, but instead sounding like she was completely into the idea that he was pitching. So, Rob decided to pounce. He spun her around, looking her right in the eyes, pulling out every bit of charm he possessed.

"So, what do you think babe, wanna fool around?" He swayed her hips back and forth, forcing a smile out of her, even if it was an unsure, uncomfortable one.

Gabby knew better, but she was bewitched by the clearing and its story. Rob was a horny dog that would probably hump her leg if she let him. If she told him no, she knew he would stop, but the thought of them not doing something out here left her feeling disappointed. She entertained the idea for a moment, trying to imagine having sex in the rough, icy snow. It seemed like a bad idea; dirty and cold, even a little gross, but it felt sexy, dangerous somehow. It was the thought of pulling apart each other's clothes, the cold air against their skin, only to have their bodies heat up again, pushing against each other in the middle of the woods where no one else can see them.

She didn't want Rob to see her considering all of this, so she smiled playfully and turned to walk away. She wouldn't just say yes and drop her pants. Instead, she would simply not deny him and see where it went.

Rob sighed, adjusted himself under his jeans, and followed her.

"Come on babe, no one is around here." And in a pitiful moment of near desperation, "I can be quick."

She laughed, assuming he was joking, and reached out for his hand.

"Let's walk for a bit."

A loud snap in the trees pulled Gabby out of the serenity for a moment, and her head turned toward the sound.

"Did you hear that?" she said, panicked.

"Probably a branch with too much ice on it, babe," Rob said, his mind squarely focused on her.

She clutched her jacket, suddenly feeling helpless out in the open. "Could it be a deer or a bear or something?"

"Nah, they'd smell your perfume a mile away. I mean I like it, but they'd steer clear of you."

He was right. Her father was a hunter and he always made sure to not shower for a couple days before going out. Aside from squirrels and rabbits, they were alone. Rob stared at her, his patience for playtime quickly wearing thin. He wanted her. He'd wanted her weeks ago when she first flirted with him. He'd wanted her this morning when she winked at him in class. He wanted her during the entire trek out here. He would have been happy to take her at any one of those places. But now they were alone and it finally felt right.

Rob grabbed her arm forcefully, but not hard, and turned her toward him.

"We're alone," he grumbled.

He shoved his mouth on top of hers, not caring that their teeth clicked together for a second. His tongue moved deep into her mouth, hers came into his. They breathed heavily, their body heat keeping them warm in the frozen field. Gabby pulled away to get one last look at him before fully committing to the act.

"Do you feel it?" He asked her confidently. All Gabby could do in response was nod. She wanted him, too. The moment felt inevitable, but it had to happen now. Right now.

Gabby took a small step back. She reached down and unbuttoned her jacket, allowing him to put his hand up her sweater. Her belly exposed to the cold, they pressed their bodies together, lips and tongues joining again. Their heavy breathing became soft moaning. She gasped when his icy cold fingers worked their way underneath her bra. Her purse fell and spilled onto the snow, but she barely noticed. Her hands went for his belt buckle and frantically unlatched it. The button on his jeans proved to be more difficult than expected. But she pulled until it came loose.

Rob's mind raced. The tryst was exactly what he'd hoped for, but now that it was happening, it felt like too much to handle, like his body would explode with so much adrenaline and desire. He squeezed all the parts of her he wasn't allowed to touch, each time prompting a bigger and louder gasp of pleasure from her. His hands worked their way up her sweater again, found her nipple and pinched it hard. She yelled out in surprise and pleasure. Her high-pitched, lustful shout sent him over the edge. Rob shoved her down to the ground, harder than he meant to. She fell backwards into deep snow.

Rob hesitated only a moment before throwing himself on top of her. He finished unbuttoning his pants and took himself out of them, ignoring the biting cold. She didn't stop him when he reached for her jeans, working to undo the three buttons at the front of them. She wanted him to rip them off, toss them aside.

His lips caressed the crook of her neck, his stubble scratching her soft skin. She looked over his shoulder, getting a good look at the clearing. It was so brilliantly bright that she'd momentarily forgotten all about the horrors that happened there. With her pants fully unbuttoned, Rob tugged and pulled them down around her thighs. That was enough for him. Holding himself up with one hand in the snow, he pulled her panties to the side, then shoved himself inside of her. She gasped loudly, not expecting as much pain as there was, but it quickly gave way to deep, warm pleasure.

Gabby thought momentarily of the condom in her purse, but the thought faded fast. There was no time. This had to happen now. She closed her eyes, soaking in every sensation in her body without the distraction of light. Rob had found a rhythm. They were perfectly in synch. They writhed and grunted and squeezed each other, both imagining that they could not possibly feel any better, then quickly finding that they could. She clung tightly to him, ignoring the wetness of her sweater and jeans.

They were so lost in each other that neither of them heard the crunching footsteps approaching from the tree line until they stopped right beside them. Gabby's eyes shot open as Henry charged toward them with a huge stick raised like a baseball bat.

She shrieked as Henry swung the wood and connected with the side of Rob's head with a sickening crack. Rob's body fell over into the snow. He was out cold. Gabby screamed in terror, but her voice barely cut through the dense forest, falling only on a few lonely birds.

Panting hard and sweating, Henry towered over

them, eyes moving from Rob to Gabby. She was lying on her back, sweater pulled up and jeans pulled down. Henry's eyes moved across her exposed body. She was flawless, shivering in the snow. A stab of jealousy stood out within the rage he was already fighting.

Drops of blood speckled her face. She looked over at Rob, still folded over awkwardly, face in the snow, bare ass pointed toward her.

"What did you do?" she screamed at Henry.

The question reminded Henry what he was there for, and he reached out to her.

"Let's go," Henry said with a touch of regret. He hadn't gotten there soon enough. Henry was disgusted with what he'd seen. But not with her. He knew that she was a victim in this.

Gabby pulled her clothes back on, "Don't fucking look at me!" she screamed, livid now that she'd had a moment to process the situation.

"You could have seriously hurt him!" her voice trembled.

Rob stirred, moaning with a stinging pain that increased every second. He lifted his head out of the snow. Blood poured from the gash in his scalp. Henry froze when he saw the damage he'd done. The whole thing was easier than he thought it would be, but seeing the bloodshed up close didn't have the intended effect on him. There was a hollowness in his chest watching Rob bleed into the snow. But Henry was quick to remind himself of what Rob had been doing, and he steeled his heart from feeling any guilt or regret about what he'd done. This asshole deserved every drop of blood lost after what he had done to Gabby.

Rob reached up to touch his scalp only to find his fingers resting on his skull. A flap of his scalp hung down by his ear. Rob stared blankly at the two of them, trying to piece everything together. Gabby realized how serious the injury was and ran over to his side in a panic.

Henry was surprised that she wouldn't take his hand.

"What are you doing, let's go," he pleaded.

"We have to get him to a hospital, Henry! Call somebody, now," she shouted at him, then helped Rob to get his pants back on. He slid his underwear up to cover his crotch, but his jeans were soaked and he was too weak to lift himself up. Gabby sobbed, doing her best to hold the loose fold of Rob's scalp where it belonged. His thick blood dripped over her fingers and down her arms. Henry stood there, bloody stick in hand, completely baffled.

"You couldn't expect me to let that happen to you," Henry pleaded.

"I would have expected you to mind your fucking business. Now call someone!"

Henry got angry. How was this going so wrong? Why was she mad at him? For saving her? All he could do was stand there, dumbfounded.

Realizing that Henry would be no help, Gabby left Rob to grab her phone from the spilled purse. In his daze, Rob didn't realize what was happening, and reached forward for Gabby's leg to keep her near him, a desperate attempt to hold onto anything he understood in that moment.

"Wait," he mumbled pitifully.

Henry saw Rob lunge for Gabby. "Stay down!"

Henry swung the branch again, this time crushing the front of Rob's face, shattering his nose, spraying blood over the snow. Gabby turned at the cracking sound and saw the horror that was Rob's face. His nose was completely smashed to one side, flat against his face, his front teeth were knocked loose, and everything from his chin to his hairline was coated in crimson. This time, Rob felt the crippling pain immediately. After letting loose a horrifying scream and spraying blood between his fingers, his fight-or-flight response kicked in. He wasn't the flight type.

Henry wasn't ready for it. He saw Rob's pain-filled rage and panicked. Rob got to his feet and tried to charge at Henry, but blood flowed into his eyes and he was still struggling to find his bearings. All he could do was reach his arms out, which was enough for Henry to hit him again, putting Rob back into the snow, writhing in pain.

"Stop!" Gabby leapt up, grabbing the stick. She felt the blood on the wood, thick as molasses, and she fought to wrestle it away from Henry.

Rob looked up and watched them struggle, his left eye socket sunken in, gushing blood, his eyeball slipping with nothing to hold it in place. Henry tried to yank the branch away from Gabby, but she held tightly to the bloody wood, letting the rough bark tear up the skin of her hands as Henry twisted and pulled. Rob wiped blood away from his good eye and saw Gabby fall to her knees holding the branch. He crawled to her, trying to help.

"What are you doing?" Henry's anger boiled over. He ripped the stick from Gabby's hands, knocking her backward into the snow, "I came here to help you!"

Rob tried to approach again, and all Henry saw was red.

"Stay the fuck down!" He raised the branch over his head. Despite how weak Rob was, or how little a threat he posed, there was no stopping Henry.

Gabby shouted, desperately, "Henry, don't-"

He swung the stick down onto the back of Rob's skull over and over again, cracking open the white bone. Rob's body fell forward. Henry kept pounding. A halo of pink and red was splattered around his head. Blood, bone and brain matter dotted the perfect white sheet of snow. Gabby shielded her ears like a child, blocking out the horrifying squish and splat of the stick mashing the brain matter to liquid.

Rob's body went limp. His face was buried in the snow, the back of his head wide open for all to see. Henry stared at his work, panting, shivering in the cold, blood pumping hard through his hands and chest. He looked down at Gabby, shaking, hands over her ears and muttering weak denials to herself. As the adrenaline slowed, it all began to sink in for Henry. He had just killed someone, a classmate. *Holy fuck, what came over me?* He'd never felt such blinding anger, or an unquenchable thirst for brutality. He started to panic. Now, he'd have to think of a plan to handle the cops.

His eyes scanned the area. Their footprints lead directly to the bloody scene at the clearing's center. He dropped the stick in his hand, suddenly disgusted with it. He hadn't realized that his palms and fingers were bleeding. The blood dripped onto the snow, adding to the smattering he'd already created. Suddenly he was terrified.

This place, Henry thought, bewildered. *It has its hands around me.* He couldn't take his eyes off Rob's mangled head. He wasn't a violent person, he couldn't make sense of this. *The clearing took hold of me, made me do this. That must be it.*

Something else dawned on him then. The clearing must have had a hold on Gabby as well. No wonder she was fighting him. No wonder she'd come out here with Rob in the first place. It wasn't her choice. The power of the clearing could make a perfect couple repel one another. It was a negative force, turning good into bad, light into dark, tranquility into chaos. A true dark spot in the cosmos. It had tainted them both.

There was only one thing to do. Get the fuck out of that clearing before either one of them fell under its spell again. He looked down at Gabby. She was still in shock, shaking from the cold and the horror, eyes locked on the hardening blood in front of her. She felt hollow, like someone had ripped everything safe and comfortable out of her, leaving her with a void in her gut, quickly filling her head with images of violence and fear.

Henry knelt to comfort her, resting a gentle – though still bloody – hand on her shoulder. Maybe this plan hadn't gone so poorly after all. Rob was out of the way and now he was going to comfort Gabby.

Henry thought of the lumberjack that had gone berserk here. He was probably level-headed and polite before he hacked people up with his axe. The murderous mother had probably been a good parent until she made the mistake of camping in the clearing. History and lore had turned them into monsters, but Henry now found himself pitying them. The power of the clearing was real.

Down on one knee, Henry tried to reason with her, to get her to at least look at him, but she was lost.

"Gabby," he whispered calmly, "we need to get out of here, okay?" She shook her head, eyes glued to the oozing blood in the snow. Her family had taken a trip to Canada when she was a girl, to a small farm where they poured maple syrup into the snow and ate it like candy. That's what the blood reminded her of. Frozen candy. She shuddered violently, trying to shake out the memory.

Henry reached out to her. "We can't stay here, it's not safe. This place is dangerous. Look what it made us do!"

Gabby pulled her gaze up from the ground. Her eyes locked with Henry's. He pulled back a little at the sight of her.

"You fucking psycho," Gabby hissed. That got him mad again, but he knew it wasn't her fault. He wouldn't let the curse, or the haunting, or whatever it was, take control of him again. He snatched Gabby's arm and pulled her to her feet.

"Come on, stay with me," he demanded as he marched her away from Rob's body, already turning blue in the cold. She kept her eyes on Rob for as long as she could as Henry pulled her toward the tree line. She knew that when she looked away, she'd never see him again.

Gabby pulled her arm back, out of Henry's grasp, and stopped.

"No, he's cold," she said.

Groaning through grimaced teeth, Henry turned back toward her, toward the body. She stood defiantly, completely still.

"If you stay here, you'll die!" he pleaded. When she still didn't move, Henry reached for her arm again. She moved with impressive speed and slapped him across the face, hard. The sound echoed and the pain in his cheek and jaw was severe, amplified by the cold.

Henry's reaction was unplanned and instant. He yelled in surprise, then reached out a hand and slapped her back, harder. Gabby's body swung around 180 degrees and toppled over, head first into a pile of snow. Her body hit the ground with the sound of clanging metal instead of soft snow and frozen earth. She cried out in shock. Henry planted his face in his hands, thinking she'd broken a finger, or shit, maybe an arm.

"Fuck, I'm sorry." He didn't know what he was doing, he just snapped. It had to be the clearing again. *God dammit*, he thought, *I had control of this, but I just slapped the girl I love across the face.* He reached down to help her back to her feet so they could finally leave, but she was holding her chest with both hands. Gabby was hurt, and bad.

Henry bent down to see what she'd fallen on. Beneath her was a huge piece of broken glass from an old window pane. She had fallen directly on top of it, and it had lodged itself deep in Gabby's chest. Blood gushed out of her wound, turning the rest of the glass a transparent crimson. His panic returned. He had no idea what to do or how to help. He couldn't remember if it was better to leave something like that in the body or remove it and stop the bleeding.

He allowed a moment of self-pity. *Why did this happen? How could I do this? What's wrong with me? She can't die, she's supposed to be mine.* But his grief and his guilt quickly faded and turned to rationalization.

I couldn't have seen that. It's glass on snow for Christ's sake, nobody would have seen that. This isn't my fault. This isn't my fault. He breathed heavily, coming down from the frantic thoughts and started to make a plan.

While he was going through his options, Gabby looked down at her chest and saw the glass sticking out of her. It didn't even hurt, really. It was so deep inside her body that it kind of tickled. There was an odd pressure where she'd never felt it before. But when Henry moved her, that's when the pain came. He tried to lift her shoulders up and away from the glass and she felt tearing flashes of cold burning inside her body. The blood poured out now, choking her and extinguishing her screams.

"Come on, Gabby. I'm gonna get you out of here."

Gabby had only a moment to consider that this was her end. She and Rob would die together in the clearing. It was romantic in a way. Not the way she would choose, but in the frantic moments before she slipped away, Gabby held onto anything happy. Those happy thoughts were short-lived as Henry planted his feet in the ground, got a good grip under her arms and pulled her body up, ripping the glass from her chest. It was deeper than she thought. It must have gone all the way through her back.

Henry dropped Gabby face up in the snow. She saw his face, contorted with effort and fear. She had known about Henry's crush on her ever since the play last year. He wasn't very good at hiding his nervousness, and she thought it was sort of cute how he got tongue-tied around her. He'd been so sweet, even just a few minutes before.

How could he do this?

She never had a chance to hear an answer to that question. The blood continued to gush. The treetops faded, the sky turned black. As she neared the bottom of whatever chasm she was descending, she made the decision to let go. She gently closed her eyes, and stopped struggling.

Henry watched her eyes drop. The tension in her

body gave way. He sat, staring at her. He'd killed her. He'd killed them both. That wasn't what he wanted. He had expected to fight with Rob, exchange a few heated words, but he thought they'd all go on their way with the situation handled. But now they were both dead. And he was responsible. Well, his hands anyway, but not his mind. He'd been tricked, had fallen prey to an ancient evil that preyed on the innocent and forced them into horrible deeds.

A plan was the first thing on his mind, but he needed time to think, to focus. Tommy would try to find him online, and he would make note of it if he was absent for much longer. His mother wasn't due back until around seven that night, so at least he had a couple hours to get home and figure out what the hell to do. There weren't many options, but he would decide on one course of action and stick to it. He felt the guilt creeping in under his heart, but he pushed it aside. No time for it, now. He would let it take him over later, down the line. In that moment, he had one goal. Get his head straight, and get away from the fucking clearing.

With one last inspection, Henry found no blood that couldn't be wiped off with a simple swipe of snow. Satisfied that nobody would stop him on the street to ask about his appearance, Henry turned away from the mangled bodies of his classmates, and marched on toward the trees. He looked up into the sky and noticed grey clouds approaching. It was going to snow.

"Good," he said aloud to himself. The tracks would be covered by morning. *At last, a spot of luck.* Nobody would think to look out here for them. At least not right away. He needed a plan, a way to make people understand that this wasn't his fault.

Without looking back, he stepped out of the clearing, instantly feeling better.

★★★

MARCH 23rd, 2018

It had been a cold and ugly start to spring, but the snow had finally started to melt, as did the momentum in the search for Rob Kipling and Gabby Martin. The entire town had come together in typical fashion with candlelight vigils crowding the high school, volunteer search parties to comb the woods, and law enforcement working overtime for the first few weeks after the teens went missing. But nothing had led to any answers.

But now, Detective Gertrude Cuthbert, mercifully called "Cutty" by just about everyone she knew, stood with her gruff, easy-named partner Glen Morris at the edge of the nearly forgotten Lawson Clearing. They watched their forensics team working on the bodies of two teenage kids. Their story had come to its most tragic end, but at least the mystery was over. Cutty wondered if people would be horrified all over again when hearing how they'd been found; naked, beaten to death in the icy cold, or if there would be a collective sigh of relief in knowing their fate. Probably both. The effects of a murder rarely dissipate with time.

"I completely forgot about this place," Glen said, exhaling cigarette smoke. He stood marveling at the sight, as Gabby had, although the view was less brilliant now. With the snow melting, the grass and dirt exposed, the place looked dirty, unfinished, and unsettled. Even the air was different. Deep in the woods, it felt pretty cold. Inside the clearing, it was too warm to keep their jackets on, but too crisp to leave them off for long.

"There used to be a path here from Spring Street," Cutty offered. "My friends and I would dare each other to get closer and closer to it. I think we got to the edge once, and that was it. Didn't realize kids today would even know about it."

"Well they got the internet, man. They know everything we knew and then some. Doesn't lead to anything good, in this old fart's opinion," Glen said, truncating his usual 'kids these days' rant.

"Oh come on, you're telling me you never tried to find a quiet place to be alone with the pretty girl in school?"

"Back of my pick up." His stupid grin made Cutty flash one of her own.

In that moment, both of them realized they'd hit the limit of humor around the scene. A little distance from the horror of a crime was understandable, helpful at times. They'd made a joke, they smiled, it was time for them to get to work.

"So, what are we thinking? They come out here for a little lover's tryst, get in a fight, maybe he gets too handsy, she fights him off?" She knew that story didn't quite fit, but it was a place to start.

Glen was shaking his head before she could finish, "Then what, she runs away after taking a few blows of her own and she trips and falls onto the glass in a freak accident?" He gave a quick, dismissive shake of his head, jiggling the flap of fat under his chin. "Nah, they're too far from each other. She realized he wasn't getting up again, she would know that based on the condition of his skull, she'd be able to slow down, be more careful with her footsteps."

Cutty nodded. Of course, that was right. "The clothes are half off a' them, both still unbuckled and unzipped. Plus, I'm bettin' that's her cell stuck in the snow over by him."

"Phone spilled outta the purse, maybe she went for it and dropped it." Glen snorted and wiped his nose with his sleeve.

Cutty's brow furrowed, thinking carefully through the scene. "So, are they caught by someone? One of the parents, maybe?"

"I can see the Dad whacking the kid's head into paste if he caught her like that, but I don't see him hurting his daughter after that, even an accident. If he was overbearing enough to kill a kid, he'd have her wrapped up in his arms until they got home."

Cutty paused, absently nodding again. "I'm liking them getting caught by someone, though, that's working." She stepped forward, deciding not to wait for the forensic team to be finished. They knew how not to contaminate the scene, and she finally had a thread that they'd been waiting months to find. She was done waiting. Glen took a last quick drag of his cigarette, bent down to put it out in the snow with a quick hiss and pocketed the butt.

They were both dressed for the cold, but still shivering. Cutty noticed that she was the only one on the scene who wore boots. Back at the station, she'd warned Glen that they'd be doing a little hiking, but he refused to believe the snow would still be deep enough to worry about. That was probably one of the reasons he was in such a shit mood. Well, that and the two dead teenagers. He cursed himself now though, knowing he couldn't complain for a second about his nice dress shoes, should Cutty dive into a big "told ya so" speech. But she said nothing about it. He was an idiot, they both knew it, no need to say it out loud. He pulled his coat tighter around himself and followed Cutty, doing his best to step inside her boot prints.

Cutty led Glen toward Rob's body, bright blue and grey, frozen solid in the unfortunate position he'd been left in, face in the dirt, ass to the sky. The state of the body was both a good and a bad thing. Good, because the decomposition was minimal, but it also took away a few of the go-to crutches they usually get started with, like establishing a time of death. They would have to consider the weather on every single day for the last few months, the possibility that the bodies could have been moved several times and dumped in this location with a single snow-storm covering the tracks, and that any cuts or lacerations they find may have been post mortem, caused by animals in the area. Time impairs all investigations, but the cold could freeze them out completely.

Todd Maker, the small town's only forensic scientist, sighed loudly when he saw Cutty and Glen approach. They were rushing him, again, but it wasn't worth arguing to keep them out for another ten minutes. He snatched a couple pairs of latex gloves from the box and handed them over. Detectives were always very impatient with his work, and he wanted to stay far away from Glen's temper. He'd heard about Glen flipping out during a routine arrest and beating the crap out of some mouthy college kid a week or so back. He didn't want to be the target of another crazy outburst with a poorly timed refusal. Keeping his eyes on the body, Todd got to his feet.

"He took a few hits before falling face first into the snow. He may have already been dead, or seconds away from it when the hits were made to the back of the skull."

"He was a tough kid. He get in any shots of his own?" Cutty asked.

"Not at all. I don't see any scuffs, cuts, bruising or obvious fractures on his hands, so I'd say he was taken completely by surprise."

"There's total visibility for acres in every direction and enough snow on the ground to slow someone's approach to a crawl. How could he be taken by surprise?" Glen said, already annoyed with him. Todd noted the annoyance, quietly rolling his eyes.

Cutty shrugged, "I'd assume his mind was on the tits in his face." She hadn't meant to be so blunt, so uncaring, but they both understood.

Everyone stayed quiet a moment, shaking their heads at the worsening scenario in front of them. Cutty glanced around the clearing, the sunlight siphoned by the trees, spilled onto the hill. The open ground, created a hypnotic pattern across the blank canvas of snow. It was beautiful, but she couldn't help an overwhelming sensation of emptiness, of unfinished business. She tried to picture someone finding a young couple having sex in the woods, consensual from the look of it, and brutally attacking them. She could understand a creep watching them from the bushes or something, but wanting to attack and kill them? It didn't make sense. Unless the killer knew them well enough to be driven to that kind of act.

"You're not thinking a random hunter walking by, are you? Something like that?" Glen broke through her little daydream with what would have been her next thought, had she not been distracted.

"It looks to me like someone was upset with him. Someone found them and attacked the boy but not the girl, at least not at first. It was the boy he was after. The girl..." She trailed off as it all clicked into place, like a picture suddenly snapping into focus.

Cutty looked at Glen with wide-eyed excitement. "He was trying to take the girl out with him. He was pulling her out by force."

"She struggled, they fight, the poor girl ended up falling onto the glass in the scuffle."

"Or he shoved her onto it," Todd chimed in proudly.

"Or he shoved her," Glen confirmed.

It worked. Cutty felt good having a tangible theory in this case, even one they had yet to investigate. It could fall apart after a single interview, but it was something to move on, which they hadn't had for months.

"I want to talk to her friends again. See if there's anyone with enough of a crush on her to fly into jealous rage."

"You think some kid did this? Seems a bit extreme for a 15-year-old." Glen said, skeptical.

"Please. Teenage boys are capable of a long list of terrible things." Cutty said, holding back a knowing smirk.

Todd spoke up again, now that he'd gotten through the preliminary examination without butting heads.

"I can't imagine how anyone can get angry enough to attack another person with your bare hands-"

"What the fuck did you say, Todd?" Glen was certain he heard judgement in Todd's voice, and it immediately triggered that old familiar feeling in his gut, that tightening, twisting anger that rose quickly, but rarely boiled over. His incident with the college kid already had the whole force gossiping, and to hear this little shit try to call him out on it made him furious.

Todd quickly tried to back-pedal. "I'm sorry Glen, that's not what I meant."

"The hell it wasn't you little four eyed fuck," Glen said, stomping through snow, ignoring his wet shoes. "I'm already paying for that shit, and what's gonna set me off even more are weasely little bastards like you out here gawking about it."

"Now listen, I didn't mean," Todd stammered.

Glen cut him off. "Shut your goddamn mouth! Unless you want a fist upside your face, too!" He took a few steps forward, raising his right fist, still scabbed over from his previous altercation.

Cutty stepped forward and rested her hand gently on Glen's forearm, careful not to forcefully pull him back. The softness of her touch was a gentle reminder of where he was in the bigger picture and he lowered his fist. He wasn't going to hit the guy anyway, he was a middle-aged nerd who had a slip of the tongue. Not worth it.

He looked at Cutty, her eyes much harder than her grip on him, and he turned back to Todd with a far different expression spread across his face.

"Hey, sorry Todd. Kinda lost my head a little there." He spoke with his most friendly voice, which was certainly forced, but sounded sincere enough. Out of necessity, he'd gotten much better at apologizing. Todd politely shrugged it off as nothing, but couldn't hide his nervous twitching.

Glen added, "I just fucking hate that. Everyone's talking about the whole incident, but no one was there, you know? People love to gossip. Drives me nuts."

With the last word in his back pocket, Glen left it there and turned toward the tree line. Cutty could have said something to settle Todd's nerves, but she only offered a polite smile and followed her partner out of the woods.

The High School was loud with activity as the detectives strolled past the gym, then the art class and the band room, all with doors wide open. Anne Michaud led Cutty and Glen through the hallways. With only a couple of months under her belt as the principle, she struggled when dealing with police. She tried to seem confident and competent when they called and asked for another round of interviews with the students, but her nerves had gotten the better of her and her voice quivered slightly as she approved the date.

Her steps were fast, heels clacking loudly down the hallway. "We had to take almost the whole week off last time you all were here. The kids were so upset," Anne said.

The cops followed calmly, routinely. They had been through the school plenty of times and knew their way around, but they could see Anne was nervous, so they allowed her to show them to the rooms and sit in on the interviews. Cutty assumed Anne would already have a few shitty kids they'd want to speak to, reestablish their whereabouts on the day of the disappearance, but resisted asking for the list of usual suspects. They would start with Gabby and Rob's close friends, as they had done during the initial investigation.

Cutty jumped right into the questions, "Was anyone more afraid than others?"

Anne tried to be helpful. "Not that I can remember specifically, but Gabby was close with a lot of the students. She was involved with the band, mathletes, drama group, basketball, field hockey. Every student and teacher in this building knew her well."

"Well we need to get started with a few questions this morning." Cutty said, keeping Anne calm.

"But, haven't you already talked to them all?" Anne wondered. "We can't do this to these kids every few months. It's too much."

Cutty shot back, "We found the bodies, ma'am. In Lawson's Clearing." Glen nodded confirmation. Anne would have to take on both cops if she wanted to hold up the interviews.

"My God," Anne muttered. "Both of them? They're both dead?"

"That's right," grumbled Glen. "So, we're gonna need to talk to the kids that go that direction on their way home."

Reeling from the awful news, she marched the cops to a much quieter part of the building to set up an interview room.

In the scarcely used Home Economics room in the far end of the school, Cutty arranged three chairs pointed toward a stool. She wanted to make sure that whoever they were talking to felt uncomfortable, put them on edge, make them understand that people were watching closely and everything they said was important. She found that being uncomfortable could help people focus.

They started with a few members of the girls' basketball team. They were all very predictable. Most of the girls started sobbing and the ones that didn't, broke down as soon as they left the room. They moved onto a few of the kids who lived in the trailer park community nearest to the clearing. There were a lot of drugs running through that neighborhood, so even while they asked these kids specific questions about Rob and Gabby, they all thought they were in trouble for something else they'd done. It was irritating. Glen hoped that one of these sketchy teens with blood-shot eyes would be shaken into confessing something they'd seen or overheard, but that was quickly quashed.

They moved onto the kids that Gabby spent the most time with; the theater kids. Glen rolled his eyes at that, knowing what was coming from that lot.

"Okay, let's just get this out of the way," Glen said, adjusting his pants, getting comfortable.

The drama kids were tougher to read, many of them had clearly rehearsed what they would say. They had nothing to hide, that was obvious, but they'd gone over this interview in their heads and their answers were all performances. Cutty relied on Glen to keep them from delivering a soliloquy about their meaningful middle school relationship with the victims and keep with the facts. He was growing tired of it, and fast.

Tommy McKenna was tapped for an interview because his house was on the other side of the woods, so most days, he walked home in the direction of the clearing. He walked into the interview room and sat down calmly, his head down, fresh tears glistening on his cheeks. He didn't want to look them in the eye. He was genuinely upset about the whole affair, shocked by it, and visibly nervous speaking about the dead. Cutty had all but written him off as just another kid, sad about his friends, until he started talking about the day Gabby and Rob vanished.

"I saw them walking down the street together. It was kinda weird."

"What was weird about it? Weren't they dating?" Cutty asked.

"Not that they were with each other, but Rob had a Challenger he liked to show off to everybody. He always revved the engines when he drove past all the kids walking home. You could set your watch to it. It was out of the ordinary for them to be walking at all."

Cutty shared a quick glance with Glen. *Out of the ordinary.* He heard it too. That phrase was the biggest and reddest of flags in an interview like this. She pushed forward.

"Anything else out of the ordinary that day? Anything at all you can think of," she probed.

Tommy furrowed his brow, trying to recall the rest of the day, but it was hazy. He knew there was something though, some other reason that day stood out. It suddenly came to him. It was Henry. Henry had been an ass that day, and he blew off their Xbox hangout to walk home.

"Did you talk to Henry?"

Out in the hallway, with all the other students waiting to be questioned, Henry sat twitching, picking at a hang nail, trying not to think about what the cops were going to ask. He had to act surprised about everything. He was sweating, breathing heavily, and he'd have to focus on making eye contact with all of them. But not TOO much. The rumor was that they'd found the bodies, but he couldn't know where, he couldn't know how.

Henry didn't look up when the Home Ec. door unlocked and Cutty stepped out. There were still a few other people in line before him. He only had a few minutes to think of what to s-

"Is there a Henry Williamson out here?" Cutty looked down to check her notes, making sure to get the name right. "Henry Williamson?"

Henry's stomach twisted in a cold knot that he thought may never come undone. They must have found something. They knew it was him, but how could that be? Nobody knew where he was that day, how could they? He'd never been a fan of Rob's, but everybody knew he loved Gabby. He should be safe.

Cutty called his name again. The other students turned their eyes to him when he didn't stand right away. The cops were waiting on him. He couldn't sit there thinking through all this shit, he was making it awkward. He got to his feet, his legs shaky with fear and Cutty waved him inside.

"Come on in, Henry. This shouldn't take long." Her smile was disarming as Henry timidly stepped into the room. The second he walked by her, Cutty's smile dropped like an anchor.

Henry sat down in front of the group, his palms already sweating. His eyes darted from person to person during the introductory questions about how he was and his relationship to the victims. He was trying to figure out what they knew, if they had anything, or if he was panicking for no reason. Either way, he was fucking this up.

Glen spoke up first, being extra certain to sound irritated.

"Henry, have you ever been to that clearing where we found the two bodies?"

"I've heard of it, yes," he said, shifting on the stool.

"I said, 'have you ever BEEN there?'"

"Uh, yeah once. It was when I was about twelve."

"What did you do there?"

"When I was twelve?"

Glen nodded, impatient.

Henry stammered, trying to find an answer that sounded like what they'd want to hear.

"I-I don't know, we, it was sorta like a dare, we j-just went to che-check it out, you know?"

"It was a dare?" Cutty chimed in.

"I mean, we went to like, test out the legend and stuff." Henry wanted to take that back as soon as it came out of his mouth.

"Which legend is that?" Cutty asked. She noted the beads of sweat forming on his brow.

Henry hesitated. The lady cop was watching him carefully now.

Take it slow, he thought to himself over and over, *take it slow.*

"You can look it up," he then blurted, trying to regain confidence but overcompensating noticeably. "Supposedly the clearing brings out your deepest desires and makes you act on them, even if you don't want to. It's one of those stupid things kids talk about."

"You think that's why Rob and Gabby went down there, to find out their inner most desires?" Glen asked with a straight face.

Henry looked over at him. Glen saw a hint of anger flash in the kid's eyes. It was quick, but it was enough for Glen to latch onto.

Henry attempted a common sense reply, "If they wanted to have sex they'd just do it. Why would they go to the middle of the wo"-

"Did you see them that day?" Glen asked abruptly, leaning forward in his chair.

Henry leaned back slightly, feeling the pressure.

"No," he managed weakly.

"No? You didn't see them at school?" Glen barked.

"Y-yeah sure, I mean at school I saw them-"

"Together?"

"I don't remember. "

"I heard you saw them after school too, Henry. Did you see them after?" Glen sounded aggressive now, almost angry at having to ask these questions.

Henry's face turned bright red. He tried to regain some composure, "No, I didn't see them after school."

Cutty pounced. "Really? Because we heard from someone who said they saw you talking to both Rob and Gabby shortly after school let out. You telling me that they were lying?"

Fuck, wrong time to take a stand, Henry thought, scolding himself. He took a deep breath and tried to stay in control, but panic rose from his spine to his stomach, tightening his chest despite his pounding heart.

He spoke calmly, "I may have bumped into them on the street."

"After school? You saw them after school?" Cutty was on the attack now. A rush of adrenaline filled her with a sense of progress for the first time in months.

"If you saw them after school, kid, then that makes you the last person to see them alive." Glen leaned back in his chair and watched Henry squirm.

Henry opened his mouth to say something to defend himself, searching for anything that would convince them that he had nothing to do with it. But it wouldn't matter. He locked eyes with Glen, then with Cutty and he saw the rabid dogs behind them, ready to pounce at a moment's notice.

That's when Glen twisted the knife. "Why didn't you come forward when we were asking for witnesses in their disappearance? You must have known that encounter would have been helpful."

Henry knew in his heart that he wasn't guilty of murder. It wasn't fair that these people would put him in prison simply for stepping onto the wrong patch of earth. Sure, he'd wanted Rob out of the way, he wanted Gabby for himself, but he would never have acted on it if he hadn't been in that fucking clearing.

Anne was uncomfortable with what was happening inside the heavy silence. Henry was a good kid, these cops were manipulating him. She stepped forward, between them.

"Okay, let's hold on for a second, here." Anne tried to sound authoritative, but nobody budged.

Glen ignored her, "I need to hear Henry's answer. Why didn't you come forward months ago when we were asking about the timeline?"

Henry didn't raise his eyes from the floor. He spoke softly, almost inaudible. "It's real, you know."

Glen and Cutty exchanged a quick glance at each other. They could both feel it. They had him. After all this time, this shy kid was going to tell them what happened to that poor couple in the woods. An electric excitement built in both of their stomachs.

"What's real?" Cutty asked, carefully.

Now Henry looked up to meet their eyes. "You don't know anything about that clearing."

Anne could see what was about to happen and tried to keep this poor kid from saying something that he'd regret.

"Now hold on, Henry. Let's just-" Anne was cut off immediately.

Glen raised his voice over Anne's, "Yeah, I know about the clearing kid, what of it?"

Henry looked up then, staring Glen straight in the eye. The fear melted away. He was caught. That made things easier, simpler. He was either going to jail, or he'd start running and see how far his legs could take him.

Building up his courage, Henry glared at Glen, "It wasn't me."

In a flash, Henry flipped over the desk closest to him. Papers and pens slid across the tile as he bolted toward the door behind him. He was already grabbing the handle by the time the cops reacted and was in the hallway before any of them stood.

Henry threw his body out the door so fast that his boots, still wet from the snow outside, slid on the tile floor and he nearly fell in front of the other students waiting to be questioned. They all jumped back in surprise and watched as Henry managed to keep his feet moving, panic keeping his adrenaline up. He barely noticed the other kids. All he saw was the light coming in through the glass doors leading to the parking lot. That was all that mattered anymore.

They had him. He was done. His only chance to escape was right then, the first moment they suspected him. So, he ran faster than he ever had, barreled toward the outside door like a bull, willing to trample anyone that got in his way.

When he got within ten feet of the door, he realized he didn't have his jacket, his hat or his gloves. It was biting cold outside and if he wanted a chance in hell at surviving in the woods, he'd have to find a way to keep himself warm. Henry lowered his shoulder and slammed into the door, keeping as much momentum as he could.

The heavy door swung open and slammed against the brick building with a huge CLANG that brought the attention of the gym class playing kickball in the nearby field. They all stopped and watched Henry running clumsily in his heavy boots.

From inside, Henry could hear voices shouting his name. "Henry, stop!" Or, "We just want to talk!" He wished that talking to them was a real option. He'd wanted to explain that he hadn't meant to kill the girl he loved or her asshole boyfriend. There was something in the clearing that made him do it, that found his weak spot and squeezed it, stoking the flame of his inner madness. What would that sound like to a cop? To a judge and jury? No, his only option was to run and hide. It would probably be for the rest of his life, but it was better than life in a concrete cell.

Henry looked back to see the whole group of cops charging after him. They wouldn't catch him. They were old, out of shape, and even though he was wearing boots, he had the stamina of a seventeen-year-old. He could at least make it to the woods and think of a plan. He looked ahead toward the tree line. The woods were far, maybe a mile from the school, but that had to be his first goal: Get to the woods.

Cutty and Glen both made it almost fifty yards from the door of the school before stopping, both panting and sweating. Cutty managed to grab her phone and put out an APB on Henry while Glen's labored breaths became an alarming wheeze. Another sign that he smoked too much, but there would be a better time to remind him of that. Once the call was made Cutty rested her elbows on her knees and joined Glen in huffing and puffing.

"We found him. We finally got that bastard," Glen muttered between gasps.

Cutty reminded him sharply, "We don't have him yet." They both looked up, watching as Henry ran full speed, directly toward the thick woods.

Hours passed. Henry had lost them all, at least for now. He assumed that the entire police force was out looking for him. Shivering quietly under the branches of a massive pine tree, Henry cried. He was scared, exhausted. He hadn't been able to think of a plan that could get him safely out of town. He had no money, no contacts, and no friends who would stick their necks out that far for him. He didn't even have his fucking jacket. He cursed himself for that every couple minutes when his body violently shivered.

He started to consider the idea of life in prison, tried to imagine his mother's face when she learned what he'd done. How could he tell her that it was true? What would happen to her with him gone forever? It was a waterfall of sad thoughts. He cried harder.

The only possible way out was to make them all understand, show them that there was something wrong in the clearing. If they could see its power, they wouldn't hate him. They would take pity on him. If they understood the effect it had on Henry, on everyone who dares step foot inside, Gabby and Rob's deaths might even be classified as a tragic accident. Once they saw, they would have to acknowledge it.

Henry forced himself to his feet, the joints in his knees creaking, his bones like icy twigs rubbing together inside his body. He looked up, trying to regain his bearings. What he had wasn't so much a plan as it was a small part of an idea, but it was all he had. He was going back to the place that caused this whole mess. He'd bring the cops there, so they could all see for themselves. Maybe they'd record the whole thing. He remembered hearing about the cops adding body cameras to everyone in the department. They could even capture something supernatural on camera, a real phenomenon for the first time ever. With that footage, he would surely be cleared of any charges. Shit, he could be famous after that, the face of the phenomenon. That idea sounded nice to him. He'd be able to explain, not only to the cops, but to the entire world, what it had been like to be completely possessed, out of control.

But they didn't understand yet. The plan could go wrong, and fast. If he led the cops to the clearing, he'd bring a lot of angry people armed with lethal weapons into the mouth of hell. If the clearing got a hold of them, they would kill him. But he wanted that understanding and that pity, so if he had to die to prove the whole thing, that's what he'd have to do.

With considerable effort, Henry started walking toward the clearing. Footsteps crunched loudly in the snow, cutting through the quiet of the woods. His breath was a dense grey mist drifting around his face, each exhale straining his dry throat. He was terribly uncomfortable. Frostbite would soon take hold, but if he could make it to the clearing, he saw a way out, or at least a way to free himself of the pain he felt, that he'd felt for months.

★★★

After Henry fled, Cutty and Glen spoke to a few more people in the school, asking pointed questions about Henry's relationship to the victims. The whole thing came together fast after that. The kids thought the story seemed far-fetched at first, but Cutty watched their faces change from "no way" to "holy shit, that makes sense" when they considered him as the killer. He'd loved Gabby, maybe he was even a little obsessed with her. It wasn't uncommon for teenagers to have trouble controlling their jealousy. But something was a little more disturbing about Henry. He'd somehow separated himself from the crime. His friends were horrified when they talked about how calm he'd been, how sad he sounded whenever Gabby's name was mentioned. It was the telling sign of a psychopath.

The largest manhunt in Aroostook County's history unfolded fast. The dogs were tracking. The choppers were in the air. Everyone in the state knew the name Henry Williamson. Cutty was confident that there was no escape for this kid, whether he died trying to survive on his own in the frozen forest, or they caught him and put him in a cage forever. She sat with Glen in the office, the two of them exhausted from a full day of coordinated efforts to organize hundreds of people for the search party. Glen closed his eyes, but Cutty was agitated, worried about the massive search.

"We need to catch him," Cutty said, mostly to herself.

"I don't think anyone's planning on letting the kid go free."

"I mean they can't shoot him," Cutty clarified when she realized that Glen was still listening. "People need to see him marched into jail wearing a jumpsuit. They all need to know that he's paying for what he's done, more than any crime I've ever seen."

"I hear ya partner," Glen offered. "But I'll tell you this, if there's a choice between stopping him with a bullet or him escaping, you can bet your ass I'll drop him. And I won't lose a wink of sleep."

Cutty left it there, not wanting to argue. But they had worked too hard to let Henry off with a quick bullet. She wanted to understand why he'd committed such a heinous crime.

Glen yawned loudly, stretching his arms out wide, ready to call it a night.

"I'm gonna hit that break room couch for a few hours," he said, finally allowing himself to relax.

Cutty still couldn't shake the feeling that there was something else they could be doing, something they hadn't covered. It was strange that they still hadn't found Henry. Police had begun combing the nearby woods between the school and the neighboring town, but found no sign of him anywhere.

Her brow furrowed, staring at a map of the town and the nearby woods. It was simplistic, with few details or landmarks noted on the wrinkled paper, but there was one distinct green circle near the center of the woods. The clearing.

"You don't suppose he'd go back there, do you?" The question left Glen confused for a second, his mind exhausted, his thoughts sluggish and fuzzy.

"To the crime scene?" The idea seemed completely out of left field, to him.

"Well, to the clearing. That's in the opposite direction of where we've been looking and it's the only significant landmark in the area." Cutty looked away from the map to see Glen's reaction. Her idea made more sense after saying it out loud, but she needed Glen to see it, too.

He stood there, mulling over the idea of Henry going back to the clearing, to where he had apparently bludgeoned his friends to death, leaving their bodies to the cold and the wolves. It didn't make sense to him.

"Why would he go back there? That kid bolted from us as soon as we were even interested in him. I can't imagine he's not still running as fast as he can toward the ocean." Glen's decisiveness made Cutty's confidence waver, but the idea still stuck.

"I'm gonna check it out, anyway," she decided.

"Ugh, why? We've got like six hundred people out there looking for this kid already."

"Right, so all the other bases are covered. What's the harm in taking another look at the crime scene?"

Glen sighed, stealing a longing glance at the couch in the break room. He looked like a high school kid staring at a girl with whom he would never dance. He turned back to Cutty and grabbed his car keys from the desk.

"Okay then, let's go," he grumbled. The couch wasn't that comfortable anyway.

Cutty smiled and got to her feet. "You sure you want to come?"

"I don't want to come at all, but if you're going out there, I should be with you, shouldn't I?" He sounded like such an indignant asshole sometimes, but Cutty knew he had respect for her. At least that's what she always told herself.

They walked together toward the door, but something important occurred to her and she looked over at her run-down, bitter and angry partner.

"Hey, are you gonna be okay? If we find him out there, I mean. Can you be cool?"

It took every ounce of Glen's control to not roll his eyes at her. But if he was being honest, he couldn't say for sure that he wouldn't beat this Henry kid to a pulp. He knew Cutty had to ask.

"I'll be fine," was all Glen said. They left it at that, grabbed their coats and headed out.

The car ride and the short hike into the woods was quiet. Exhaustion was setting in, slowing them down, but they'd first have to scratch this itch first if they expected to get any sleep. The idea that Henry would come back to the clearing had begun to make more sense to Glen as they made their way through the thick woods. The sun was on its way down, so the flies were out now, buzzing around their eyes and ears, testing the limits of Glen's patience. Way too tired to handle this shit, he could feel his anger building.

"Here we go," Cutty said as she spotted the tree line. She stepped into the clearing and took a deep breath. The air smelled fresh, but felt thin. She felt lightheaded when she stepped into the open field. Behind her, Glen lost his balance and stumbled as he stepped into the clearing with her.

They saw him at the same moment. Henry sat on a stump with his back to them, still, silent, hunched over. Her first thought was that they needed to call for back-up. They were all alone out there and to bring him back alive, they would most certainly need help. Cutty reached down and unsnapped the strap on her holster, freeing her sidearm, should she need to pull it quickly. *Alive*, she thought to herself, *we take him alive.*

Glen followed suit and they exchanged a quick glance of disbelief. Cutty grabbed the radio from her belt and kept her voice low as she called it in. *Should have done it before.* She'd been stupid and impulsive and now here they were, the killer in their sights and they were unprepared. They'd get their back up, but for the next few minutes, they were alone with a murderer.

Glen made sure to stay quiet, "Let's take him, now."

Cutty nodded and they moved forward, approaching Henry with great care. She didn't think they'd be able to surprise him, but she wanted to be close enough to where she could shoot him in the leg if he tried to run again.

"Alive, god dammit," she whispered sternly.

Henry remained motionless while the two cops crept up behind him, but when they were about twenty feet away, Cutty stepped on a large branch, snapping it with a dry crack that echoed through the clearing. Henry whipped his head around in surprise. He leapt up and spun around to face them, prompting Cutty and Glen to both pull their weapons.

"Don't move, Henry!" Cutty shouted.

Henry put his hands up, instinctually.

"I'm not gonna run!" Henry tried to explain, but they wouldn't stop barking orders at him long enough to listen.

"Get down on the ground! Now! Get down!"

"Face down!"

"Keep your hands up!" The yelling was almost involuntary. The adrenaline was pumping through all of their veins now.

Henry watched the situation escalate and thought to himself, *this is it. The clearing is taking control. They want to kill me, and they will.* Henry kept his hands in the air, but he refused to lie down. The second he did that, it was over. They would shoot him without understanding what happened. The cops' faces turned red, the veins in their necks and foreheads bulging, spittle flying from their mouths with every shout. He needed a chance to explain. He waited for them to take a breath and with as much force behind it as he could muster, he shouted, "Stop!"

Henry tried to keep his cool. Cutty and Glen both stopped shouting, guns still drawn. They were both panting loudly, waiting for Henry's next move.

"I-I needed you to see it and get that this place is real. Can you feel it?" Henry asked.

Glen was quick to respond, "You need to shut up and get your face in the dirt, before we unload on you, kid."

"That's it, right there. That feeling." Henry seemed almost relieved that it was happening. Soon, they would see it, and they'd know what happened to him.

"Tell us what you did, Henry," Cutty muttered.

"We were all here, the three of us. The clearing took them first, made them... do things." Henry closed his eyes and shook his head, trying to wipe the image of Gabby and Rob fucking out of his mind. "I saw what was happening, that she'd lost control of herself, so I tried to stop it. She couldn't have known what she was doing. But when I got here, the clearing had gotten its teeth into me too, and I hit Rob, hard. It's not what I wanted to happen."

"And what about Gabriella? How did she end up impaled on that glass?" Cutty threw back.

"I told you, none of this was what I wanted. Gabby was an accident. You have to understand; this place is evil. It makes everyone evil. It was my hands, but wasn't me."

Cutty was baffled. Was this kid trying to set himself up for an insanity plea? "Henry, however it happened that day, you need to come with us."

"You can explain yourself at the station. You'll want to have your lawyers there," Glen chimed in, making no effort to hide the contempt in his voice.

Henry shot back, "No! You have to see it for yourselves. No one will ever believe me if I tell them in a prison cell. Do you know the story of this place? The axe murderer, the mother who killed her children, and now this. It's all the same."

"You're damn right it's all the same, kid. Get your ass on the ground, now." Glen's patience was wearing thin, and fast.

"Easy, everyone calm down," Cutty pleaded.

Henry grinned. "You're getting mad, aren't you? You feel that? It has you. Soon you won't be able to fight it."

Glen's face grew redder. He did indeed feel the fire of anger ignited inside of him. The audacity of this kid, this murderer. The more he said, the angrier Glen got. It was that familiar feeling he was trying to avoid, the same one that got him into trouble with that damn college punk. But if he messed this one up, the consequences would be far worse. His hand quivered with restraint, rattling his sidearm.

Cutty could see her partner struggling to hold onto his temper. They were so close to catching the killer they'd been seeking for months. All they had to do was hold it together, make this arrest properly, and get Henry back to the jail. Easy.

Trying to keep things calm, Cutty said, "Henry, explain it all to us on the ride back. We'll listen to you, okay? It's freezing out here, there are hundreds of people on their way. Let's just have a chat over some coffee, okay?"

"Don't fucking talk down to me! You're not listening!" Henry's face contorted with sudden rage. His cheeks were flush. He was nearly out of breath as he shouted. "This place makes you do things that you wouldn't normally do. I'm a good kid, I get good grades, I'm on the varsity track team. I would have never hurt Gabby like that!"

"But you did," Glen barked.

"I'm sure you'd never murder someone in cold blood, right? But that's what you're thinking now, isn't it? I can see you want to shoot me. You want to see my brains all over the snow. Go ahead, fucking shoot me."

Glen's hand shook, his rage fighting to make its way out of his body. He did want to pull that trigger, to shut this kid up once and for all, then go to sleep knowing justice had been served. He could do it, too. Cutty wouldn't rat on him. All Glen had to do was fire.

Henry could see the conflict on Glen's face and he stepped forward. Cutty warned him to stay back, but Henry had already accepted the fact that he was going to die here. There wasn't another way out of the clearing. He took another step toward Glen.

"Do it, you fucking pussy. I know you want to. It knows your weakness." He stepped forward again.

Cutty saw what was about to unfold. Either Henry would grab the gun or Glen would shoot him.

Henry was almost within reach now. Cutty considered shooting him now, too.

"You believe it," he spoke only to Glen, "I can see that you believe me."

Glen was shaking, grinding his teeth, using every bit of energy to keep his finger from curling and pulling the trigger. Henry stepped right up to the gun, ready to die. Cutty saw that look, that familiar curl of Glen's lower lip, the same thing she saw before he punched the college kid.

She made the decision to stop Glen. As she reached out to grab his arm, Glen suddenly stopped shaking. A calm came over his face. Henry saw it too and paused. He flipped the gun around in his hand and offered it to Cutty, butt first. She snatched it as Glen grabbed Henry with both hands and shoved him back, away from the guns.

Henry was surprised when Glen routinely pinned his arms behind his back and closed handcuffs around his wrists.

"You have the right to remain silent," Glen began, his voice surprisingly calm, with a hint of smugness.

Henry turned his head, trying to look Glen in the eye, but with Glen's knee in the small of his back, he wasn't able to move much. Glen continued to recite the Miranda rights while Henry grappled with what had happened. His stomach lurched as he realized he'd been tricked. He had been foolish to think that they would believe him. Maybe this is what the clearing wanted.

"Kill me! Go on you mother fucker, I know you want to!" Henry shouted at Glen.

As he finished reading Henry his rights, Glen grabbed Henry's neck and lifted him to his feet, looking the kid square in the eye.

"What kind of animal would I be if I let myself do whatever I wanted?"

Henry made a last attempt to plead with Glen, to make him understand that he was a victim. "But this place, it pulls the evil out of you, whether you want it to or not."

Cutty stepped forward, both weapons away now and spoke to Henry matter-of-factly. "Hey kid, everybody's got a reason. Not everyone does it."

Henry shook his head, frantic. He tried to struggle, but Glen had a hold of him. He wasn't going anywhere. "No! It wasn't me! And it wasn't Gabby, she wouldn't have done that."

His anger turned to sadness and fear when he heard the repetitive thump of the approaching chopper overhead, the police sirens spill into the clearing, and the bark of dogs following his scent. He'd lost. His eyes darted back and forth like a captured stray animal, looking for anything to reveal the sinister force at work. An ancient Native American symbol, a Wiccan pattern on the ground, a fucking Swastika carved into a tree trunk, anything he could find that would show that there was evil in this place.

But there were only trees, wind, leaves, dirt and grass. The clearing was suddenly nothing more than an empty space in the woods, earth and air like the rest of the world. The pit in the middle of Henry's stomach deepened. Maybe he should have killed himself out here.

Cutty and Glen both held Henry's arms and marched him out of the clearing. Approaching the edge of the trees, Henry was sure that the feeling in his stomach would subside as soon as they stepped past the tree line. It had to. A horrible mixture of guilt, embarrassment and self-pity consumed him, but it was only a result of his time spent in this wretched place. He'd start to feel better the second they stepped out of the clearing. They reached the edge and Henry closed his eyes to cross the threshold. He couldn't stand this feeling another second.

But when he walked out into the woods, he felt nothing, no change. The clearing was a few yards behind them now, but nothing felt different.

Confused, Henry marched forward, still stuck with the dread and sickening guilt in his gut. As the police loaded him into the back of a squad car, Henry began to realize that he might feel like this forever.

One thing was for sure though; none of this was his fault.

THE END OF EDGAR WREN

E very time I go to sleep, I imagine my own death.

Every night.

Without fail.

Before I drift off, I wonder how I'll go. *What's finally gonna get me?* Before my eyes close, I run through all the ways I could be killed before waking up. You'd be surprised how many there are: carbon monoxide poisoning from the ancient heater in the living room, a fire started by the downstairs neighbors cooking on their tiny hot plate, a building collapse after the massive earthquake that we all know LA has coming, my wife sleepwalking and shoving a knife through my throat. The list goes on.

The most common scenario I imagine is someone breaking into the house. The method in which they murder me changes night to night. If they barge in with guns, there's not much I can do. It's over quickly. I'd barely have time to wake up before they put a bullet through my face. The idea of a knife is painful, more terrifying, but at least they would have to be within arm's reach and I'd have a fighting chance.

Being tied up and tortured is a possibility, too. I imagine a group of men tying my wrists and ankles to one of the kitchen chairs with duct tape, pulling out my fingernails one by one and cutting off small pieces of me until I finally bleed out and they leave my lifeless body in the living room until the neighbors complain about a terrible smell. Although I don't think I've got enemies strong enough for that. And the people in this neighborhood are more likely to grab my Xbox and run than face anyone in the house. Even so, every time I click off the bedside lamp, I listen intently for the sound of glass breaking, of wood splintering, of footsteps down the hallway.

Every night.

Without fail.

I'm afraid.

I know I'll die from something senseless and stupid. I try to steer clear of staircases when I can. If I'm not paying close enough attention, I could lose my footing and tumble face first onto concrete. I'm clumsy, I've got big feet, it's more than possible. If a neighbor found me at the bottom of the stairs, skull crushed, blood everywhere, people would find out what happened. Months of investigations, physics tests, an autopsy, maybe a court case, only to conclude that I'm a fucking uncoordinated idiot that tripped and lost his life.

That's what scares me the most. Something pointless. A life spent for nothing. That's the thought that shakes me, keeps me awake longer than usual. The idea that thirty years of choices, problem-solving, education, and relationships led to absolute zero. Life is not meant to end that way.

As I fall asleep, I go through the checklist. Did I lock the door? *Yes.* The deadbolt, too? *I think so, better check.* Is the window closed? *It'll bring sweltering heat and the living room will be a sauna in the morning, but it's closed.* Won't matter anyway. If someone wants in, they can break the glass. They can bust the lock on the door, too. It's cheap. The fact of the matter is, if someone wants in while I'm asleep, I'm done for. So is my wife, sleeping next to me. If the roof collapses on top of us, we'll be buried under a pile of steel and concrete. Not much to do in that situation. If one of the police helicopters circling our neighborhood loses power mid-air and crashes through our window, what can we do?

When I finally go to sleep, my dreams uncover extra

creative ways to die, like a crack in my helmet while deep-sea diving, falling into a pool of lava. Those are less likely, but it could happen. And I can't shake that sinking feeling. That vulnerable, helpless, hopeless waiting. I'll die eventually. Something *will* get me. Hopefully not soon. But it could be soon. It could be right now. Tonight, could be the end of Edgar Wren.

Of course, I'm at the mercy of death in the daytime, too. I'm no stranger to daylight fear. But there are distractions that occupy my mind throughout the day. I coordinate reports for a small tech corporation, so essentially, I pass emails from one person to another. My job is hard, tedious. It keeps me focused with small daily goals that give a false sense of progress and purpose to my life. I desperately wish I did something else for a living, but that seems pretty normal. Most people hate their jobs, hate their families and want to die. Only time I think about death at work is when I want to kill myself from boredom and repetition.

Not like I'd actually commit suicide, though. I've thought about it, considered the ways in which I'd off myself, but they all take too much initiative, too much ambition, too much commitment. Although I must admit, it's comforting to know how you're gonna go. It's nice to think you could have some say in it. I'd probably poison myself. No, maybe shoot myself. That's quicker. Probably painless. I'm definitely not a cutter. That takes serious balls. And it's inconsiderate to boot. Someone has to clean up the bloody mess you'll leave. But no, I wouldn't commit suicide. I'm not brave enough. I'm sure I'll die in an accident or in my bed as an old man. Or cancer. That's the slowest, the saddest... I hope it's not that.

Lying in bed next to my wife who has no idea the darkness in which I'm wallowing, I close my eyes and work to slow my worried mind. I brush off the day's burdens and open myself to the quiet calm of the dark bedroom. I live in a nice place. It's big, open. The ceilings are high. The paint is fresh, still vibrant. We moved in a couple of years ago and we're not sick of it yet.

We're happy, Shelly and I. Happy enough for me to fear a death that would cut our relationship short. If someone breaks in, kills us both in our sleep, we'll miss out on things we're excited about. Kids we might have, trips we might take. I want to know what we're like as old people. I imagine we'll be funny. Well her anyway, not so much me. I'll be bitter, cranky. Maybe I'll be ready for death then, but not now.

With a random jolt of energy, she clicks on her bedside lamp, rolls onto her side and casually asks me how I want to die. Either she's reading my mind, or there's something morbid swirling in the air, infecting us both.

"I want to drown," she says before I can answer. "I've heard that drowning, after the pain, is supposed to be calming."

"That can't be true," I tell her.

She gets annoyed and asks again how I want to go. I don't like that question, never have. There's no good way to go. Maybe dying of an orgasm that's too powerful? Even then, that sounds kinda horrifying. You die because your body stops working. That's either painful, disorienting, or instantaneous. None of those sound appealing.

I roll my eyes, tell her that I'd rather not die.

"I'd like to see the end of the universe with my own eyes, watch the sun blink out and feel the last of its light on my skin before everything dissolves into permanent blackness."

She says I'm no fun, I'm not playing the game right. We argue about it for a few minutes before rolling over to go back to sleep. She's got my mind racing again. What if I died now? Would she care? Would she be happy? Thrilled that I'm out of her hair? I do most of the work around the house and I make all the money. If I died now, she'd have a hard time living on her own.

Though to be fair, the opposite would be far worse. I'd be helpless. If there were a crazed killer in the room with us who brandished a weapon, I'd plead with them not to hurt her. If I wasn't able to stop him and she was killed, I would miss her terribly. I would probably want to die, myself. Maybe then I'd consider suicide. Probably the poison.

I look over at Shelly's back. She's pushed the covers down to knees and cuddled her extra pillow, her usual sleep position. My eyes scan down to her ass, tucked neatly into tiny pajama shorts. After eleven years, I'm still attracted to her. She has curves. When we have sex, I can grab her all over. She feels amazing, and soft. If she were killed in an accident or shot to death in her workplace parking garage, I would never feel those curves again. I'd think about them, long for them. Even if I were getting over Shelly by sleeping with someone else, I would feel the difference, and it would shatter me.

That's what's in my head as I roll to my side of the bed and get comfortable. It's a good life we have here. I'd hate to lose it. Thirty years I've been working toward where I am. Where we are together.

The idea of dying now is terrifying.

The morning is a little happier. I sit at the dining table over a plate of toast and eggs, staring out the window at the ominous grey clouds. I force myself to ignore the terrible news blaring from Shelly's tablet on the countertop and block out the thought of a nuclear blast going off downtown. That would brighten the grey sky, for sure. We'd both be blinded, then disintegrate in a split second. Gone without a thought. Nothing left. At least a murder has a body, a representation of what you used to be as a person.

I put on a pot of coffee, careful not to drip any water on the power strip. That could start a horrible electrical fire.

I fix up some toast for Shelly and it makes me think of choking. Similar to her idea of drowning, but with no chance of that calming she mentioned. I add a little extra butter and blackberry jam. Can't have the toast too dry.

In the bathroom, I look down at the floor. This building is old. We love it, but it's old. A small pipe connector for a gas heater sticks out of the wall, never removed since the 1920s. It sticks about three inches out from the wall, four inches off the ground, and it's been painted over a million times, so it matches the ugly yellow color of the walls. It's at the perfect height to trip someone. If it does, it'll send them spilling into the dresser, which has sharp corners. I try to get Shelly to move the dresser, but she won't. She doesn't understand, doesn't see the danger in it. I call the landlord and tell him to remove the pipe. It's a hazard.

He says, "No."

He says, "Be careful."

The morning commute is the worst part of my day. It's only a ten-mile drive, but there are too many people around me on the four-lane roads. All in big metal wreckers. All in a massive rush. Both my hands grip the wheel, knuckles clenched and white. I check every intersection carefully. Inspect every crosswalk. I flip my tie over my shoulder to make sure it doesn't get tangled in the steering wheel. I exaggerate every lane change to avoid surprising my fellow commuters. I'm relentless with the blinker. I often use it when I'm the only person on the road. If anyone kills me in a crash, at least I'll have the comfort of knowing that it wasn't my fault.

The traffic is terrible today. Bumper to bumper. Seems like every single person is running late. But I'm not. I never get over fifteen miles per hour in the city. A crash probably won't mean death for me. Minor injury. Insurance headaches. That, I can deal with.

Behind me, I see a flash. A motorcycle flies through the traffic, splitting the lanes. That's legal now. The bike weaves through the cars without slowing down. I imagine the rider losing their balance, hitting a sideview mirror, control of the bike slipping from the rider to gravity. I picture it flipping out from under him, the metal exhaust scraping the asphalt, pouring a wave of sparks into the street.

I see the bike jam itself beneath my car, igniting the gas tank underneath, wedging my door closed, trapping me inside. The smoke seeps into the cab. I'm choking. I cough violently as my body tries to resist the acrid air. The car gets hotter, my skin sweats like a faucet, clothes stick to my skin, the flames surround me, engulf the car from the bottom up, blocking my view of anything outside. I can see only fire. I'm in hell.

The motorcycle whips past me in a blur. I snap back to reality, back to my driver's seat, shaken, but safe and sound. The rider stops in front of me. After all that, he didn't even catch the light. My blood is pumping. The veins in my neck throb with each heartbeat. And with each pounding beat, my anger rises. The audacity of this man. To put all these people in danger like that. I doubt if he even knows. Or cares.

I kick open my car door and let it swing as I stomp through the parked cars toward the rider. I'm only a step away when I realize I have the tire iron in my hand. I'll make sure he thinks the next time he wants to go bombing through the streets. Teach him what it means to be considerate of other people on the road.

I scream an involuntary, "Hey!"

I admit, it's not much of a warning.

He turns. I see the man's shock through the visor before I bring the iron down on his shoulder. I feel his bone break. He shrieks and falls off the bike. It topples over with no sparks.

I hit him again and snap his collar bone in two. The

stoplight turns green. Nobody moves. They all watch from their cars, jaws dropped, horrified. But the audience won't slow me down. I bring the iron down again and again, hitting whatever part of his body I can reach. He holds his hands up, stupidly protecting his face, forgetting his helmet. I wail on his ribs. By the time I stop, the rider is unconscious. Maybe dead. There's no blood, but he lies in a heaping mess on the ground. I feel better. My blood stops boiling, and my heart slows. We're all safe for now.

The people around me are on their phones, shooting video or making calls. They look afraid of me. Idiots.

I shout, "He almost killed me!"

They don't understand.

I get back in my car and work my way slowly through the vehicles stopped at the intersection and head off to work. Cars shouldn't stay parked at a green light. It could most definitely cause an accident. Possibly a fatal one.

I realize I may have gone a little overboard. But my point has been made. I will not be killed in a stupid, senseless traffic collision. I could take the bus, avoid situations like this in the future, but that increases the chances of getting knifed in the back by a drug-addled vagrant looking to snatch my wallet. No, I'd rather be in control. My car, my choices, my insight. I'm careful. I'm safe.

At the office, I sit all day, staring at the screen, waiting for the police to show up. I know they'll come. And when they do, I'll explain myself.

There are plenty of everyday dangers to worry about, even in this nice comfy office. We're on the eleventh floor of a building that's always filled to capacity. It sways in the wind and feels like it will snap in half when the Santa Anas kick up every fall. It won't. But again, this is California. Earthquakes are serious. This building is newer. It's built on underground rollers to allow the building to shift and move if there is a large quake. That's a comfort, but if the building does come down, I'll be one of the thousands killed or trapped under the rubble.

If that happens, I want to go quickly. I can imagine what it'd be like to suffocate, breathing in only dust and dirt for days with my limbs pinned under a million tons of glass and steel. I'm claustrophobic too, so, the thought makes me shiver.

At noon, I do my usual rounds to check all fire exits in the office. I make it look like I'm going to the bathroom or stretching my legs, but I'm actually going through the hallways to check each of the six fire doors and make sure there's nothing wrong. I keep my eyes down to avoid eye contact with everyone I walk past. People ask questions if they catch me doing my own safety check.

I head to the stairwell door nearest to my desk. The knob

turns. The door swings open. Perfect. I move down to the other side of the office. When I turn the corner of the tight hallway, I find a huge mess of boxes. The fire door is blocked. I stop dead in my tracks, arms dangling by my sides. My jaw drops when I find the office manager, a bull-headed man named Nelson, unloading more boxes, blocking the fire exit further. The freight elevator is near the fire door and I realize that Nelson is doing his job the lazy way.

"Nelson," I demand, "you're blocking the fire door."

"Just for a minute," he replies, without a fucking care in the world.

"If there's a fire right now, you and I will be trapped-"

"I don't have the patience for you today, Edgar. If there's a fire, feel free to knock this shit over and make a run for it, okay? I'm not gonna be here more than five minutes, unloading this." His tone makes it clear that he doesn't take me seriously. Must be nice to go through life so care-free and happy. Fucking hippie.

I read him the riot act, "I will not burn to death because the fire door isn't clear, the way it's supposed to be."

Raising my voice, I remind him, "There are loading bays for this sort of thing."

He rolls his eyes as I explain the dangers of unexpected objects at the top of a long staircase. Not only could I trip and fall, break an ankle, crack my skull open, but everyone behind me, rushing to get to safety, could also trip, and together we would tumble down the metal steps, breaking arms and legs along the way, unable to outrun the encroaching fire. Another horrific, avoidable way for us all to die.

Nelson says nothing. He scoffs and turns to walk away, not giving the boxes another thought. He's on his way to the boss's office, I'm sure. Probably to tell her that I'm causing trouble again. Nelson and I have a history of getting into it. He seems over it today, unwilling to fight back, like he usually does. That means I've won.

So, I start clearing the door myself. I lean down and pick up the boxes. No idea what's in them, but they're heavy. I plop the first one down with a loud metallic BANG. I couldn't care less if the contents are breakable. I'm just hoping they're not explosive.

At the sound of the boxes being shuffled around, Nelson rushes back around the corner.

"Hey," he shouts, "don't touch those! That's expensive gear in there."

"Then get them out of my way."

I'm ready for round two.

Nelson charges at me down the long hallway, stomping like an angry kid whose younger sibling is playing with their sacred toy. I lift another box and set it down hard, on top of the first one I moved. He looks like he's going to hit me. I don't step up to him, but I don't cower, either. My chubby gut can take a punch.

In defiance, I reach for another box.

He gets to within arm's reach and pulls the box away from me.

"I told you not to touch these." His voice quivers with anger. He shoves my shoulders back. I stumble back a couple feet. When he leans down to pick up the boxes, he slides them to the side and flings open the heavy fire door.

"See," he turns to me and shouts, "now if there's a fire, everyone can leave. Consider yourself up to code, you fucking lunatic."

My blood boils again. The audacity of this moron. He blocked the fire exit and he's upset with me for telling him I don't like it. He should know better. He's the damn office manager; the fire code is his responsibility. If he's not paying attention, I guess it's up to me, as per fucking usual.

He continues to bark at me, but the words are meaningless. I focus on the open fire door and the stairwell behind him. I don't know why he can't see the same heap of charred bodies I do. They're all too real for me and I can't ignore them. Nelson needs to learn what the risks are. Either he doesn't know or doesn't care.

I tune back into his rant, hearing, "... you need to calm

the hell down with this shit. You can't worry all the time about what might happen to you-"

I speak calmly over his ranting, "Do you realize what a trip down those stairs could do?"

"The fuck you say?" His brow furrows. He doesn't understand me.

I take three huge steps toward him. Nelson thinks I'm going to punch him and he blocks his face. Instead, I plant my shoulder in his gut.

My old football training kicks in. I remember how to tackle. I lift Nelson off his feet and throw him backward, through the door.

I try to shove him toward the flight of stairs, but his resistance throws me off. He tumbles backward and he flips over the railing, feet whipping up into the air as his body falls down the center shaft of the eleven-story stairwell.

He has only a second to scream before he hits another railing on his way down. That silences him. His body thuds and splats as he tumbles like a broken doll, bouncing from metal to metal.

I look over and see his body land with a shockingly loud SMACK on the concrete of the bottom floor. He is almost liquid now. Blood drips from every surface his body hit on the way down. I can track his fall with ease. Certainly, not how I would have wanted to go.

I step back into the hallway. I'm relieved. This feels right. It feels like it was inevitable.

Nelson's been responsible for my life and every life in the office for the last eight years. Who knows where else he was cutting corners? Did the smoke alarms even work? Was there enough water to get us through a week, if we get trapped in here? What's the structural integrity of these fucking glass walls around the offices? How could those possibly be safe? Jesus, there are a million things I haven't thought of, I've done these people a favor by ending this careless, destructive man's reign.

I close the fire door without a sound. I saunter back into my desk and gather my things. It's late enough for me to sneak out without people noticing. I'll say I've got a doctor's appointment if anyone asks. They won't. Only the jangling of my keys grabs anyone's attention, the bright young assistant that sits next to me, but her eyes move immediately back to her screen and stay glued to it. I take the back way to the elevators. Can't chance the boss seeing me.

Someone else steps into the elevator with me. An old woman desperately clinging to her youth. Her suit is tailored and stylish, clearly expensive, her makeup is excessive and elaborate, her cheeks covered in a mountain of foundation, her floral perfume so thick you can almost see the cloud surrounding her. I roll my eyes. This is not the person I want to die with if this elevator gets stuck or if the cable snaps and we both plummet to the ground.

I'd rather go out alone.

In the car, I make sure to calm myself, slow my heartrate before driving. Even though it's not yet rush hour, I don't want to drive through the city all riled up, then find myself in another confrontation in the middle of the street.

The police must be looking for me. I want to go home, sleep a little if there's time, then hit the road. I'm tired as hell, but going to sleep now is an obvious risk. What if the cops break down my door while I'm napping on the couch? I'd panic and jump to my feet, ready for a fight. They'd no doubt shoot me full of holes before I could even register what was happening. They'd probably shoot Shelly, too for good measure.

I haven't decided where to hideout yet. Probably some town I've never heard of. Somewhere completely random, so the authorities won't even know where to start looking for me. I can steer clear of them. I only need to stay diligent.

When I get home to collect a few things for my trip, Shelly's red, puffy eyes say that she's been crying. I set down my bag and toss the keys in a drawer. The usual routine.

"Honey?" I ask every question with the one casual word.

She struggles, but mutters through a wave of sobs, "Did

you have a fight with someone on the way to work this morning? A man on a motorcycle?"

I sigh loudly. I explain the near crash, the possibility of burning to death. She waits for me to finish my explanation. I can see it does nothing to settle her mood.

"That man is in the hospital. You broke both his collar bones, his arm, and ruptured a disc in his spine. How could you do that?"

She isn't sad, she's angry with me. I wish I could make her understand the danger I was in. I try to tell her, to explain my reasons for not wanting to die in a fire, but she can't let go of the violence. She's traumatized. I get it. She's never been violent in her life. Never felt like she had to be.

There's nothing else I can say. I need to leave before this gets worse. She tells me the cops called her and told her about the incident. They're on their way here to talk to me.

I'll pack a bag, hop back in the car and drive out to the desert somewhere, make a plan from there. A twinge of sadness creeps up behind my eyes, flooding my sinuses, and making my eyes water. Part of me hoped she would come with me. It's useful to have a second person when on the run.

Maybe once she calms down and understands why I did what I did, she'll join me, wherever I end up.

I want to hug her, to say a proper goodbye. I don't want this to be our last conversation in case I'm killed in a crash during a high-speed police chase. One step forward is all I manage before she grabs a knife from the kitchen sink and holds it out at me.

Stopped in my tracks, I stare at her, baffled as a chill pulses through my gut. I wasn't ready for an altercation, not between us.

Her voice trembles and cracks as she yells, "Stay away!"

My eyes don't leave the knife in her hand. It glimmers and shines. She grabbed the biggest one of the bunch. I know how sharp it is. A couple of days ago I went through and sharpened all the knives, myself. That one cut through a pumpkin with ease. And now Shelly swipes the air in front of me, accenting every command with a swish of the blade. She doesn't understand how dangerous that is.

Her words become wind as my mind centers on what might happen here. She's scared. She thinks that she needs to defend herself. Any move I make to reassure her is met with another swing or a jab in my direction.

If she catches me with that sharpened edge, it'll cut through my skin like a scalpel. If I reach for her and she lashes out, she could sever the veins in my wrist quickly and efficiently. I'd bleed out in about a minute.

How sad would she be then?

Plus, she'd have to clean the whole mess in the kitchen and I know she wouldn't want that. Even if she was pissed at me, even if she knew about both incidents today, she would be annoyed if she had to clean puddles of my blood from her kitchen tile.

I start thinking that she could cut herself by accident.

"That's sharp," I proclaim, thinking it will make a difference.

It doesn't. Shelly sobs harder.

I come closer and she's faced with the idea of actually stabbing me. The more afraid she is, the more I want her to know that I won't hurt her. I wasn't planning on it, anyway. But this is spiraling out of control. She's bound to hurt one of us if she's not careful.

I lift my hand, my fingers reach out to caress her cheek, to comfort her.

"Babe it's oka-"

I hear the knife's whip through the air as she swings it with both hands, like a baseball bat. She catches the inside of my bicep with the fiercely sharp blade.

I feel the pinch of unfamiliar pressure on thin skin, then the stinging pain as my flesh is exposed to the air. Blood drips down the front of my shirt in heavy gobs.

She's cut me deep. Not the artery, I don't think, but I can see muscle under the skin. The pain is exquisite and intense. I grab her wrists and shake the knife loose from her hands. It clangs on the ground, bouncing loudly on the recently tiled floor.

Now, Shelly panics.

I squeeze her wrists hard. I want her to stop, to listen to me, to calm down. She's put us both in danger. I'd never put her in danger like this. Not if it could be helped.

Shelly fights. Her mouth opens wide, crooked with pain and fear. She tries to yell my name, but instead a guttural scream shakes the room. The neighbors will hear this. My blood pumps, my heart pounds, my control slips away. I won't be a husband who gets murdered by his wife. Never. W e're happy, Shelly and me. But she's acting crazy.

I scream in her face, "W hy are you doing this?"

Through pained sobs, she manages, "You almost killed somebody."

I scream again, louder. "As a matter of fact, I almost killed somebody, then I <u>did</u> kill somebody. And you know what? W e're all the better for it. I could have been killed a million ways today. Did anyone bat a fuckin' eye?"

That doesn't calm her down. My arm throbs as the skin tears. Shelly tries to wrestle her wrists free, but I don't let her go. If I let her go, what's to stop her from stabbing me again just for good measure? I could be dead in the next few minutes if I don't protect myself.

I shove my wife backward. Her feet slip on the slick bloody tiles. Her head hits the corner of the counter so hard that the toaster jumps. A thick trail of blood smears from the countertop and over the cabinets, following the back of her head. She's down but not dead. Knocked out cold. With her head tilted at an awkward angle, she snores loudly.

I didn't mean for that to happen, but it's probably for the best. She could have died from that hit, but I can't decide if that's okay or not. I freeze in place, watching her blood trace the tile grout and mix with mine. Our new kitchen floor is now red.

Lights flash outside. The cops were quick. There must be a dozen of them. All for little old me. Shelly opens her eyes. The snoring stops. With effort, she lifts her head. I can see that it's painful. Regret begins to stifle my anger. My blood cools.

Shelly looks at me, her memory slow to return. I stare back, waiting for the inevitable realization of how she ended up on the ground, covered in blood. Her eyes go wide, she sees the red mess on the ground and she gasps.

The cops pound with angry fists and the front door rattles on its hinges. They shout for us to let them in. I won't open it for them. They'll have to fight their way in.

Shelly hears them too, but in a daze, can't get to the door. She screams. Her voice is so loud that I leap back a step.

My heart thumps in my chest again. Her scream is wet, blood-soaked, desperate. I can't stand to hear it for another second.

Glass shatters behind me. The cops come in through the window. Shelly keeps screaming. I put my hands to my ears and try to focus, to make sense of what's happening. I don't want to die in this chaos. I need to die in silence, in peace.

Shelly screams louder.

When her breath runs out, she sucks in a lung-full of air and screams again.

That's all I can take. I can't have this insanity anymore. I grab the knife from the ground and jam the blade into the small of Shelly's throat. I hit her vocal chords and keep pushing it through to the top of her spine. She stops screaming.

The shock in her eyes fades into nothing, her chin rests on the knife's handle before she goes completely still.

I'm finally able to take a deep breath and steady myself.

But the calm is short-lived. It's not three seconds before a cop grabs me, presses my face onto the bloody tile floor and cuffs my hands behind me, while screaming something about lawyers and the things I say. I get the gist of it.

Despite my limited visibility from the floor, I see the officers clear the rest of the house, moving through it tactically to see if anyone else is here. Orders get shouted, communication is clear. They're good. I'm not going to die here after all.

These cops are by the book and they've got their man red handed, dead to rights, all sewn up. I don't give them a reason to shoot me. They yell commands in my ear. I'm happy to follow and obey.

I feel warm, weirdly okay, and for the first time in a long time, I feel safe.

★★★

My head rests on a thin pillow, my body on the tattered mattress covered by cheap plastic. It makes a loud crinkling noise every time I turn over. The lights in here are harsh, bright, and they buzz so loud I can hear it in my dreams.

They've painted my walls again, this time a nice calming tan color. It looks washed out in the bright fluorescents, but I like the change. Before, it was a pretty pale blue, but that got old real fast. The cell is on the smaller side, about 8x10 feet, but I find it to be cozy. It's not cold, like I expected a prison cell to be, but the air tends to get humid from time to time, the floor and walls get a bit damp, but it's an even trade, I suppose.

With a loud KA-THUNK, the lights on C Block, Death Row, go out for the last time. Tomorrow is my day. At twelve o'clock noon they're going to lay me down on a gurney that's probably more comfortable than this damn bed, strap me in, show me off to a small audience, give me a moment for last words, and fill my veins with poison that will put me to sleep forever. Most guys are nervous to know their fate in such detail, but not me. There's a delight in knowing exactly how you're going to go. It's no longer left to the imagination. In a tiny prison cell, there are people on staff who won't let you die. It's their job to keep you healthy, keep you comfortable and calm until the day they take you into another room to kill you.

Strange occupation. I hope it pays them well.

I spent so many nights up late, pondering the possible ways my body could be mangled and destroyed. It could have been an intruder, a car accident, an earthquake, a murderer, drowning, a plane crash, a fucking piano falling on my head from a high-rise window. At long last, my thoughts aren't racing with bloody hypotheticals. I know exactly what's going to happen to me; they've already walked me through it.

But of all the ways to go, I never guessed I would prefer an execution. Honestly, it seems like the best way to go.

Guess I've finally got an answer for Shelly's stupid question.

THREE SCREENPLAYS

I began my writing career as a screenwriter, and after ten years working myself half to death, it was time to look back at the work I'd done. With dozens of completed features, shorts, TV pilots and scores of unwritten ideas, I had a solid collection of stories of which I was immensely proud. But anyone in the world of movies will tell you that writing for the screen can be a slow, frustrating endeavor, and of those dozens of stories, less than five had been produced, which meant that only a small percentage was seen by an audience, making the stuff I had in my back pocket feel like a waste of words on my hard drive.

Of course it feels that way, because in and of itself, a script is an unfinished work, no matter how many drafts you've completed, or rounds of notes have been addressed, or how rich the characters are or how well the story structure works. Until someone hands you a pile of cash to take it into production, a screenplay often feels like a blueprint for something to be built by other people down the line. But I've read many unproduced scripts that conjure beautiful imagery and hit hard with emotional storylines, with great language that's distinct and precise, even poetic. Those scripts were a delight to read. They were done by terrific writers. I'd read them again. I'd recommend them to friends. I'd buy them in a book store.

A screenplay, a good one at least, is much more than a simple list of action, description and dialogue. A comedy is hard to sell without well-written jokes; a thriller's suspense can't be built without proper stakes; and action films become monotonous and boring if we don't understand their characters. That old Hollywood saying remains true after more than a century of cinema, "You can make a bad movie from a good script, but you can never make a good movie from a bad script."

In 2016, I submitted to a well-known writing contest called *NYC Midnight*, an organization that has year-round writing competitions, covering a wide range of storytelling mediums with several challenges for each. I was most intrigued by the short screenplay contest, a timed challenge in which each writer receives three prompts – character, subject, and genre – a time limit, and a maximum page count. It was a test of storytelling agility and would help to hone the skills to create memorable, impactful stories with short form screenwriting. But it was tough. And there was stiff competition.

More than 1,100 writers submitted to the challenge that year, so I didn't expect to make it very far, but after surviving all three rounds of competition, I landed in 4th place overall. I was absolutely thrilled, not just for the recognition and top five placement, but the three short screenplays that came out of it are clever, fun, and well-executed. The whole experience is a perfect example of pressure and limitations breeding creativity and originality.

I decided to include those scripts in this book for a couple different reasons:

First, more selfishly, these are stories that would never have seen the light of day under normal circumstances. The ideas are too focused to be TV pilots or features, and they're too expensive to be produced as short films. I was faced with shelving them all for good. I didn't like the idea that people would never know these stories exist. So here we are.

Second, I hope readers can connect with these stories

the same way they'd connect with any short fiction. So, maybe the next time you curl up in bed looking for something to read, you'll consider a good script instead of a novel. Because these are not just blueprints for the future, these are stories that exist here and now, ready to be consumed by readers.

During the challenge, I was given eight days to write *Nylah's Magic*, three days for *Electric Detective*, and just twenty-four hours to finish *The Red Helping Hand*. Because the time limits were so integral to the creation of the stories, I haven't gone back to rewrite them since they were completed. What follows is exactly what was submitted for each round of the contest.

Enjoy!

- Billy Hanson

NYLAH'S MAGIC

EXT. GREEN FIELDS - NIGHT
A stunning green field has turned blue in the moonlight. The air is quiet and still, only the grass moves in the breeze.

A single, lonely wagon appears, making the huge trek across the plain, pulled by two horses. It moves slowly, quietly toward the mountain range in the distance.

INT. WAGON - NIGHT
Inside the wagon, NYLAH (9), peeks out through the wood, watching the land go by. She's worried about something lurking out there in the dark.

Nylah is smarter than most girls her age, but always afraid to let herself shine, keeping herself shy and quiet.

Behind her, a baby wakes up starts to fuss. She moves to her newborn baby brother, JORDY as he begins to cry.

NYLAH
Shh, we must be quiet now,
Jordy.

Her voice is gentle and sweet, but the baby continues, louder and louder.

Nylah looks to the front of the wagon. Her father ERRON and mother ELLA have their backs to her, steering the horses.

Two unlit torches hang on the outside of the wagon. Ella looks nervous and tired.

ELLA
How much longer, Erron?

ERRON
Shouldn't be more than a couple of hours. If no one's found us by now, we're likely in the clear.

ELLA
Somehow, I don't think so.

IN THE BACK, Nylah quietly closes her eyes and gracefully waves her hands in front of her, casting a spell.

The back of the wagon begins to glow with a soft purple color until the light is focused into one spot in front of her. The light slowly shifts into the shape of a small dragon.

Waving her hands to control it, Nylah makes the dragon fly and twist through the air in front of Jordy's face.

The baby stops crying and starts to smile. The dragon dance is beautiful, and Nylah and Jordy both start to laugh as it floats like a kite toward the roof, then dives down at them.

From the FRONT OF THE WAGON, Erron turns at the sound of his kids playing. His face is tired, worn-down. Erron is a kind and gentle man, beaten down by circumstance.

His face hardens when he sees the small purple dragon.

> ERRON
> Nylah! Enough!

She spins around, caught red-handed, and looks ashamed.

EXT. GREEN FIELDS - NIGHT
On top of a hill, overlooking the entire plain, a group of five KNIGHTS sits atop their horses, watching the wagon move.

From their vantage point, they can see the purple light coming from inside the wagon blink out in a flash.

Their leader, BARD (45), speaks with a booming voice.

> BARD
> That's it. Let's go.

He rides off toward the wagon and the other knights follow.

INT. WAGON - NIGHT
Erron crawls to the back of the wagon.

> ERRON
> I told you nobody can see that
> until we cross the mountains!

> NYLAH
> I know, but the baby was
> crying.

Erron softens. Jordy smiles up at him, melting the anger away instantly.

ERRON
(Smiling)
Well, he's not anymore.

Nylah keeps her eyes down. Erron puts an arm around her.

ERRON (CONT'D)
I know it's hard, Nylah, not allowing yourself to be free. But that's why we're leaving. To make sure that you'll always be safe.

NYLAH
How come we're not safe at home?

ERRON
There are some people who think that you want to hurt them. They're like your Mummy and me, they don't have any magic, so they don't understand it. They're just afraid.

NYLAH
But my magic can't hurt anyone.

ERRON
I know that dear, but they think all magic is dangerous. And some of it is. But it

doesn't matter, we'll soon be
free of them.

NYLAH

But if people wish to hurt us,
can't we fight them?

ERRON

If you're smart enough to see
a fight coming, you should be
smart enough to avoid it.
Good and kindness can always
triumph without a fight.

Erron puts a hand on her head, comforting her and earning a
smile. The moment is broken by Ella's worried voice.

ELLA

Erron!

He snaps up and runs to the front of the wagon.

ERRON

Nylah, stay with your brother.

AT THE FRONT of the wagon, Ella points out into the
dark night. Five torches move toward them, the distant sound
of hoofs ahead of them.

ELLA

They came out from the
valley. They must see us from
there.

ERRON

Could be traders.

ELLA

Could be.

They wait. The torches move closer until we see armor.

ELLA (CONT'D)
(Terrified)
Erron? What do we do?

He hesitates.

ERRON

Let me do the talking.

EXT. GREEN FIELDS - NIGHT
The five KNIGHTS charge up to the wagon. The metal clashes and clangs and the wagon rolls to a stop.

The knights surround them. Bard speaks with terrifying authority.

BARD

Step out of the wagon, all of
you.

ERRON

Will you permit my boy to
stay inside? He's not yet six
weeks old-

BARD

All of you, out!

Erron nods back at Nylah. She scoops up her baby brother and the family hops out of the wagon, facing the knights.

Bard steps off his horse, still towering over them.

ERRON
What can we do for you, sirs?

BARD
Your name?

ERRON
Erron Balfour, sir. My wife Ella, daughter Nylah and my son Jordy.

BARD
Will you deny crossing the plains to enter the Arbor Lands?

ERRON
No sir, that's where we're headed. My Uncle has work for us out near the Capital City.

BARD
I assume you've got papers.

ERRON
Of course.

Erron pulls a rolled up piece of parchment and hands it over. Nylah trembles and keeps her eyes down.

BARD
And why are you headed there in the dead of night with a newborn and no torches?

ERRON
Well we tried to leave earlier,
but had too much to pack.
Lord knows the women
couldn't let go of anything in
the house. And honestly sir,
I'm so bleedin' tired I didn't
even notice the torches had
burned out. Been riding for
hours tryin' to keep my eyes
open.

Bard looks up from the parchment, unimpressed. Nylah lifts
her eyes to the men on horses, but quickly looks away when
one of them catches her and looks back.

BARD
This all looks to be in order.

He hands the parchment back.

ERRON
On our way, then?

BARD
I see just one more problem. I
saw your wagon movin' across
the field, middle of the night,
no torch, quiet as a mouse,
which is suspicious enough.
But then I seen a light comin'
from the back of it. A purple
light that don't exist in nature.
A light that could only come
from magic-

> ERRON

Surely, that couldn't have been us.

> BARD

I saw it with my own eyes, boy! And don't you dare interrupt me again.

> ERRON

Apologies sir, we saw no purple light. And it says on our papers, we've tested as non-magical.

Bard ignores him and looks down to meet Nylah's eye.

> BARD

And you, girl? How old are you?

> NYLAH

Nine, sir.

> BARD

And have you done your tests yet?

Nylah shakes her head, nervously. Erron hangs on every word.

> BARD (CONT'D)
> Waiting until you're ten, ay?
> Pushing it right to the limit?

Nylah looks to her father, desperate. All he can do is nod.

> BARD (CONT'D)
> And when do you turn ten?

> NYLAH
> Five days.

Erron's heart sinks. He tries to do some damage control, but just sounds desperate.

> ERRON
> We figured since we'd by in the Arbor Lands by her birthday, we didn't need to have her take the tests–

> BARD
> You open your mouth again before I address you and I'll drag you back to the Capitol in a bag.

Erron stops. Bard leans down, eye to eye with Nylah.

> BARD (CONT'D)
> Can you do magic, sweetheart?

Nylah shakes her head, no.

> BARD (CONT'D)
> You know that all magicians must be reported to the King, yeah? They can be very dangerous if allowed to go free. Are you dangerous?

Nylah shakes her head again. Bard stands up straight.

> BARD (CONT'D)
> Nah, you don't look
> dangerous.

That hangs in the air for a moment, everyone waiting on pins and needles for his next move.

Suddenly, Bard whips his sword from its sheath, raises it above him and swings in down to strike at Nylah. Ella leaps forward, but she's too far.

> ELLA
> No!

Nylah reacts, throwing her hands up in a panic. She unknowingly releases a streak of bright purple.

Bard's sword stops before it would hit her. His face lights up with a smile. His plan worked.

Erron immediately tries to interject.

> ERRON
> Sir, please. She's only a girl.
> Her magic is only spectral,
> she's no danger. Please.

Bard slams the hilt of his sword into Erron's gut, doubling him over and dropping him into the grass.

Jordy begins to fuss again, in Ella's arms.

> ELLA
> She's our child, sir. Please
> understand. We want no
> trouble.

BARD
I understand that you were taking your illegal child across the border, into a country we will be at war with inside a month. I understand that's treason and punishable by death for all.

Nylah has tears running down her face, not sure what to do.

NYLAH
I'm sorry, mother.

BARD
You can't hide who you are, girl. You come with us.

ELLA
No, please! Nylah!

Bard steps toward Nylah and she turns to run. Another knight is there to stop her and she's trapped.

Bard snatches her hair in one hand and pulls her back to his own horse. Jordy begins to cry louder with all the noise.

BARD
(to his men)
Bind her hands, throw her on the back of my horse. And kill these traitorous scum.

ERRON
Sir, I beg you for mercy.

Jordy cries louder, starting to scream. One knight ties up Nylah's hands. She struggles, but stops when she sees the baby wailing.

> NYLAH
> Mother! The baby's crying.

> ELLA
> Don't struggle, Nylah.

> NYLAH
> But you can't let the baby cry!

Bard steps toward the family, raising his sword again. But for real this time. He intends to kill them all.

Ella crouches down, shielding the baby. Jordy screeches, louder than any baby has ever been able to scream.

A massive crack of thunder rips through the sky and the clouds flash with RED LIGHTNING.

> SCARED KNIGHT
> Did you see that?

As the thunder rumbles, they all stare up at the clouds, unsure of what happened. Jordy continues wailing. Bard puts two and two together.

> BARD
> Grab the newborn!

The VIOLENT KNIGHT steps toward Jordy, but Erron leaps forward and shoves him back.

The Violent Knight slams a fist into Erron's face, knocking him back down, spraying blood over the grass.

Jordy lets loose another massive wail.

The thunder cracks again and the sky glows red, stopping them all in place.

Nylah looks up to see the light is coming from a huge red figure in the sky. They all watch it slowly descend through the clouds. It's a creature of some sort, falling with grace.

As it moves toward the ground, Jordy screams again and the figure opens two sprawling wings and flies at the knights.

It's a DRAGON. A massive, red dragon that looks exactly like the dragon that Nylah made earlier, aside from the color.

> SCARED KNIGHT
> It's coming for us!

The red dragon swoops down at the Violent Knight just as he pulls a knife and reaches for Erron. The dragon screeches and closes its jaws around the Violent Knight.
It lifts him into the air and drops him with a metallic CLANG! The knights all stare as the red dragon flies into the sky again.

> BARD
> Run! Now!

The knights try to gather themselves to flee, but they're all scared. They ride out in a group, leaving the family behind.

Erron and Ella watch in astonishment as the dragon floats in the sky above them. It's a stunningly beautiful sight. Their eyes drift down toward their baby, still wailing.

Nylah is on the back of Bard's horse. She tries to wriggle off, but Bard holds her there, hopping up onto the horse.

BARD (CONT'D)
You're staying with me.

Bard rides off, trailing the group of knights.

The dragon swoops down from the sky again, wailing in anger. The knights all scream in fear as the dragon flies at them.

It hits the group, knocking them all off their horses, spilling them onto the ground, armor smoking from the heat.

Bard sees them all out of the fight and he turns and charges back toward the family. His eyes are on Jordy.

Above them, the dragon howls and spins in the air, the same way Nylah's dragon did. Then is swoops down toward Bard.

Erron and Ella see the horse coming toward them. They try to quiet the baby, but Jordy is still wailing.

ELLA
Jordy, please. Shh.

Erron watches as the dragon glides downward, coming at Bard's horse from behind. Nylah looks behind her and sees the dragon approaching, its face angry.

Thinking fast, Nylah raises her hands as best she can and casts a quick spell, throwing a bolt of light in Bard's face.

BARD
Aarrgh!

He yanks the reigns and the horse bucks, throwing Nylah and Bard to the ground. They both roll to a stop.

Ella gets to her feet and climbs into the wagon with Jordy.

ELLA
Nylah!

Bard gets to his feet and charges toward the wagon. Nylah sees the dragon coming and keeps her head down, allowing it to swoop down, just above her.

The dragon opens its jaws again, aiming for Bard. He does his best to run in the armor, but it's nothing to match the speed of the sailing red dragon.

It clamps its jaws onto Bard's leg, throws him up into the air. His sword drops and he screams in terror as he starts to fall. The dragon opens its jaws again, now beneath Bard.

The screeching knight falls right into the dragon's mouth. Nylah watches as Bard falls through the dragon and slams down on the ground with a metal thud.

The dragon screeches again and leaps into the sky. Not finished. Nylah runs quickly over to the wagon.

NYLAH
Father!

ERRON
Nylah, come quick!

Jordy continues to wail. Bard writhes in pain on the ground.

Nylah runs into her father's arms. Ella holds the baby and tries to quiet him, but it's no use.

ELLA
Jordy. Please stop!

The dragon circles. Erron sees it swoop again and dive down, coming right for the wagon.

> ERRON
> Ella, stop him.

Jordy wails. The dragon approaches.

> ERRON (CONT'D)
> Ella!

> ELLA
> I can't!

Nylah turns and sees the dragon coming at them. Ella desperately tries to rock Jordy.

> NYLAH
> Father, untie my hands.

> ERRON
> Nylah, run!

> NYLAH
> Untie my hands!

Erron pulls a knife from inside the wagon and begins to cut her ties. He frantically saws through them as the dragon gets closer and closer, Jordy screeching louder.

Finally, the rope splits, freeing Nylah's hands.

In SLOW MOTION, Nylah turns to face the dragon, now only a few yards away. She holds her hands one on top of the other.

Before her, a thin, shimmering field of purple light appears in front of her. The dragon flies directly into it, changing its color from red to purple as it passes through.

Nylah, now with control of the dragon, sends it spiraling upward, then brings it down slowly to rest on the ground beside them.

She moves her hands slowly, making the dragon lie down like a tired dog. After a moment, everyone watching in awe, the dragon begins to disappear and Nylah drops her hands.

The air falls silent and Jordy's crying finally softens. Nylah steps into the wagon and helps her mother comfort the baby. Erron and Ella are both stunned, in awe of her.

> NYLAH (CONT'D)
> It's okay Jordy, we don't need
> to be afraid anymore.

From behind her, Bard speaks through the pain.

> BARD
> Those children must be
> destroyed!

Erron moves to speak, but Nylah rests a hand on his shoulder. She speaks to Bard, standing on the wagon.

> NYLAH
> I am not dangerous. But you
> are. It was you who forced us
> out, and you who attacked us.
> You should hope that my
> brother does not remember
> that when he is older.

With that, Erron snaps the reigns and the wagon moves. Bard manages to raise his head long enough to see Nylah staring back.

She waves a hand gracefully as she pulls away, casting one last spell. Next to Bard's face, a small flower, made completely of purple light, grows and blooms.

Scoffing loudly, Bard watches as the wagon rides off.

FADE TO BLACK.

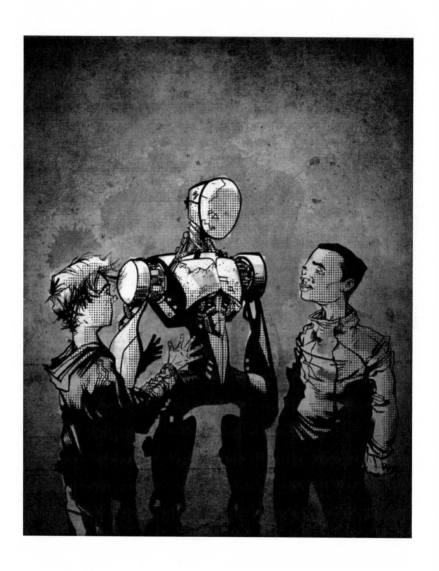

ELECTRIC DETECTIVE

EXT. RUNDOWN MANSION - DAY
A large house stands in the middle of a dusty, dirty field.
Broken machinery and scraps of metal litter the area like a
junk yard, but this was once a beautiful house.

The front door flies open and boy of 12 rushes out, mad as
hell and storming off. TONY is bright and witty, but has a
huge chip on his shoulder that he won't ever shake.

He grabs a bike from the porch when a huge man, GUS,
charges out behind him, yelling. He grabs Tony's arm and
holds him.

GUS
Hell you think you're going?

TONY
Meeting up with Derek.

                    GUS
        You got chores to be doin'.

                    TONY
        You're not my father, Gus.

Tony yanks his arm free and hops on the bike, speeding off, kicking up dust behind him. Gus yells after him.

                    GUS
            That's right, I'm your boss.
            You work for me and in this
            place that means I own you.
            You signed the papers boy,
            what's done is done!

Tony pedals harder, barreling into a trail in the woods.

EXT. ABANDONED BARN - DAY
Tony now pushes his bike, walking slowly next to his friend DEREK. He's a good kid if you ignore his smart-ass side.

They pass a decrepit, abandoned barn on the verge of collapse, surrounded by a field, left untended for decades.

                    TONY
            I can't stand Gus anymore. He
            thinks he owns the whole
            county.

                    DEREK
            He kinda does, man. But I
            hear ya, though. My boss tells
            me the same thing and he just
            owns a water pump. It's
            stupid, really.

TONY
He reminds me every single
day that when the bombs fell,
he made the most money, he
was the big shot.

DEREK
Well that's only because
before the bombs fell, there
was other shit to do besides
scavenging.

TONY
I doubt he'd do well in a
world like that–

Tony trips on something and falls on his face. Derek nearly
falls himself, he laughs so hard.

Behind Tony there's a small, shiny piece of metal poking up
out of the dirt. It's smooth, like polished chrome.

DEREK
The hell is that?

TONY
I don't know, but if it's a car
part then I can bring it to Gus
and he might lay off me for a
bit.

Tony starts digging, shoveling the dirt with his hands and
revealing something much bigger. The metal piece he tripped
on is the undamaged skull of a robot.

DEREK
Holy shit.

Derek kneels and starts digging with him, revealing more and more of the human-sized robot.

They find its entire body, still covered in clothing. Once it's completely uncovered, Tony and Derek work to pull it out of the ground.

Both friends just marvel at the thing for a moment, stunned into silence. The robot is made entirely of the smooth, chrome-like metal. Its face has no features, just a blank shape where eyes, a nose and a mouth would be.

> TONY
> It's completely intact.

> DEREK
> It's got all its fingers and toes, that's amazing.

> TONY
> What is this doing here? This isn't even a mile from Gus's place and he's had scavengers dissect this area looking for any kind of tech they can find. This should have been found years ago.

> DEREK
> You know what, we should get it in the barn, out of sight. We don't want anyone passing by and seeing us with this. They'd just as soon shoot us as split the finder's fee.

TONY
You're right, come on. This is
gonna make us a fortune.

They grab the robot and start dragging it toward the barn.

INT. ABANDONED BARN - EVENING
CU on a flashlight shining directly at us. Once the light
moves, we see MAX, a 14-year-old girl with more technical
skills than anyone twice her age.

MAX
Where'd you get this?

DEREK
We dug him up right outside.

TONY
We need to figure out more
about him if we're gonna sell
him, you know?

MAX
Well, he's a city bot, I can tell
you that. This kind of tech is
expensive, man. Wait, did you
check for the battery pack?

TONY
I don't know how to take this
thing apart.

Max scoffs, rolling her eyes. She reaches around to the back
and snaps open a small panel, but it's empty. No pack.

                    MAX
Damn, already gone. That
would have made you guys
some real money.

                    TONY
What do you think it was used
for?

                    MAX
I'd say it's a police-bot.

                    DEREK
Shit, really?

                    MAX
Well there's 'NYPD' stamped
on it and it has what I think is
a gun slot on its right thigh.

                    TONY
Oh shit. If this thing is a cop
and it's been buried in the
ground, do you think it was
working a case in our town?

The other two share a moment of realization.

                    MAX
Makes sense. Wanna ask him?

                    DEREK
You just said this thing didn't
have power.

Max digs around in her bag for something. She dumps out a
few random pieces of scrap, including a bulky taser.

> DEREK (CONT'D)
> Whoa, what's that?

He tries to touch it, but she bats him away.

> MAX
> That's just in case you annoy me.

> DEREK
> Okay, jeeze.

> MAX
> These police units have an alternate input so they can work if their batteries are damaged. But only during the daytime.

She pulls out a small gold dish.

> TONY
> This thing can run on solar power?

> MAX
> If it still runs at all. Hey we gotta try. If there's a criminal in our midst, we should know it.

Max has already started hooking the dish up.

> MAX (CONT'D)
> Here we go.

She flips a switch inside the battery opening and there is a quick PANG as the CPU boots up.

                    DEREK
            Oh my god, it works.

Suddenly, the robot's head begins to move, it's arms begin to shake, and its legs start to stretch. The kids all stand in awe as the robot steps off the table and stands.

They stare at it blankly. The robot looks each of them over, scanning them, waiting for one of them to speak.

                    TONY
            H-hi.

                    ROBOT
            Good evening, citizen. I
            apologize, it seems that I was
            powered down incorrectly.
            Would you re-orient me?

                    MAX
            It's May twenty-first, 2356.
            You're in a town called
            Falmouth, Maine.

                    ROBOT
            Falmouth, yes. My memory is
            coming back online. My name
            is Detective Silver of the
            NYPD.

                    TONY
            So, you were a cop.

ROBOT
I was and still am an officer of
the NYPD, yes.

TONY
Listen buddy, I don't know
how to break this to you, but
there is no NYPD anymore.
It's all gone. After the bombs,
the world just dried up.

Silver twitches slightly, trying to process the information.

ROBOT
I must attempt to finish my
current objective. There is a
violent criminal in these parts
and he must be apprehended.

DEREK
How long you been down in
that hole, copper?

ROBOT
Approximately eleven years
and two months. My memory
seems to have been corrupted,
but I believe that before I
could approach the suspect, I
was ambushed, my battery
unit taken and I was buried so
I could not receive solar
power to reboot. You have
my thanks for reviving me.

DEREK
Then your suspect is probably long gone anyway, man. We can find another use for you.

ROBOT
I will then need confirmation of suspect's apprehension before moving on to a new objective.

TONY
Well, maybe we can help. What's the name of your suspect?

ROBOT
The name is one Gustave McKenna, of New York City.

Tony's eyes go wide. Derek and Max both gasp.

DEREK
No. Effing. Way.

ROBOT
Do you know this name?

TONY
I do. And I can do you one better.

Tony grins.

EXT. RUNDOWN MANSION - SUNSET
Tony pounds on the door of the house, obnoxiously loud.

                    TONY
            Gus! Get out here, I got some
            salvage for you!

                    GUS (O.S.)
            Just bring it in then!

                    TONY
            You'll want to see this outside.

Gus grumbles and stomps over to the porch.

                    GUS
            What is it that so important?

                    TONY
            Before I show you what I've
            got, can I ask you a quick
            question?

                    GUS
            Tony, I don't have time for
            this.

                    TONY
            How'd you make your
            fortune?

                    GUS
            Scavenging, you know that.

                    TONY
            It wasn't because you came
            across a high-tech battery unit,
            was it?

Gus freezes, understanding. The sun continues to set.

> TONY (CONT'D)
> Because my friend here thinks
> you may owe him an
> explanation.

Tony steps aside, revealing Detective Silver near the bottom of the stairs, gun pointed up at Gus.

> GUS
> Son of a bitch. How'd you get
> out?

> ROBOT
> Gustave McKenna. You are
> under arrest for murder and...
> stri...

Silver trails off. Tony panics and looks back. The sun is setting behind the trees and Silver is powering down.

Gus grins, shoves Tony out of the way and snatches the gun from Silver's limp hand.

> GUS
> Thought you were clever you
> little prick? I've been just
> itching for a reason to put you
> in the ground. Now I've got
> one. And I know the perfect
> spot.

Gus aims the gun at Tony, ready to fire. But suddenly there's a CRACK! Gus starts to convulse, being electrocuted. He drops the pistol on the ground and falls over, shaking wildly.

Max stands behind Gus with her taser. Tony snatches the pistol up off the ground and Max finally lets up.

MAX
That was fun

TONY
Thanks Max. Soon as the sun
comes up, we'll get Detective
Silver to get rid of him. Derek,
tie him up.

GUS
Think you can stop me, kid?
Tony leans down, eye to eye with Gus.

TONY
Sorry Gus, what's done is
done.

Tony steps over to Silver, slips the pistol back into the hip
holster and walks back inside.

FADE TO BLACK.

THE RED
HELPING HAND

INT. DEL'S BEDROOM - EVENING
This room hasn't been lived in very long. Just unpacked boxes, bare walls, a bed and piles of clothes.

The door room flies open and DOLORES "DEL" MABRY (13, bright but full of unstoppable hormonal rage) charges in, furious. Her long hair has been freshly dyed a bright BLUE.

Her mother, CARLA MABRY (40s, you can see where Del gets her temper) stomps in behind her. She throws the empty box of blue hair dye on the ground.

CARLA

Del, you're supposed to be
finishing your school work,
not dying your damn hair.

DEL

You can't keep me locked up!

CARLA

Well, I wouldn't have to home school you if you would stop acting out so much. Get your act together and we can talk about you going back to school. This situation isn't easy for either of us.

DEL

Dad wouldn't care if I dyed my hair, Dad would let me go to school and Dad wouldn't keep me locked inside the house all day!

CARLA

You want to go live with your father? You get some money, you get a plane ticket and you can go out to stay with him. Until then, you finish your assignment.

Carla slams the door behind her.

Del throws herself onto her bed to have a good, frustrated cry when suddenly there's a light KNOCK, KNOCK, KNOCK, a rapping of knuckles on wood. Del looks around, confused.

She walks over to the far wall and moves a large box to reveal a tiny wooden door, about the size of a dog door. Del leans down, taking a closer look at it.

A KNOCK, KNOCK, KNOCK comes from inside it. Cautiously, Del reaches down to the lock and slides the dead-bolt free. The tiny door swings open, sending Del backward in surprise.

> DEL
>
> H–hello?

Out of the darkness, a HAND slowly emerges. A right hand, wearing a dark red leather glove, a pale, scaly white arm behind it. It presents itself to her with one gentle wave.

> DEL (CONT'D)
>
> Mom–?

The hand snaps up and motions for her to STOP! Scared, Del freezes. The hand stretches its fingers, the leather glove creaking and crackling, preparing itself for something.

With a graceful twist of the wrist, the hand grabs a neatly folded piece of paper from thin air like a Vegas magician. It holds the paper out for Del.

Del stares at it for a beat. Reluctantly, she takes it, unfolds it. Her brow furrows. It looks like her school work.

> DEL (CONT'D)
>
> But this is–

Carla pushes the bedroom door open again, cutting Del off.

> CARLA
>
> Did you call me? What is it?

She stares at Del, waiting for an answer. Del looks to the tiny door and sees that it's now closed. No sign of the hand.

>   CARLA (CONT'D)
>   (RE: paper)
>   What's that?

Bewildered, Del hands the paper over to Carla.

>   CARLA (CONT'D)
>   Oh, you did it already.

Carla look it over quickly, pleasantly surprised.

>   CARLA (CONT'D)
>   Good. See, told you it would
>   be quick. Just had to do it.

Carla hands the paper back to Del and leaves.

Del turns back as the tiny door opens again. The red right hand returns. It rotates slowly, turning the palm up and wags the fingers like a beggar asking for change. It repeats this GIMME, GIMME motion until Del understands.

>   DEL
>   You want something?

The hand turns, extending one finger to point at her chest. Del looks down to where it's pointing. Her necklace.

The hand turns over. GIMME, GIMME.

>   DEL (CONT'D)
>   Fine, it's old, anyway.

Del takes off the necklace and places it in the hand. The fingers close around it and the arm pulls back, into the strange black abyss beyond the door. Looking at the paper in her hands, Del gets an idea.

> DEL (CONT'D)
> Wait! Can you get something
> else? I need to get out of this
> house. Can you get me
> money?

The hand returns, stretches its fingers again, knuckles cracking as it prepares another trick. Del watches anxiously.

With another graceful wave, the hand whips a folded wad of cash seemingly out of thin air. Del's eyes go wide and her jaw drops. She snatches the money out of the hand.

> DEL (CONT'D)
> Oh my god! Is this real? It's
> real!

The hand turns over. GIMME, GIMME. Del looks around the room, searching for something else she can sacrifice. She goes to her bed and pulls a small jewelry box from underneath.

She sets it proudly into the palm of the red hand. It holds the box for a moment, then throws it aside with a loud CLANG! Then GIMME, GIMME.

> DEL (CONT'D)
> Hey! What do you want,
> then?

The hand crooks one finger, beckons her toward it. Carefully, Del leans in close, like it's going to tell her a secret. The hand gently reaches up and strokes her hair. Del pulls back.

> DEL (CONT'D)
> You want my hair? I just did
> this.

GIMME, GIMME. Del resigns herself, grabs a pair of scissors from a box, and stares at them in her hand, unhappy.

> DEL (CONT'D)
> Maaaaaan.

She lifts the scissors, holds her pony tail tight, and with a few heavy cuts she takes off most of her new blue hair. With a big frown, she sets the hair down in the hand.

She runs a hand through her short hair then starts counting the cash. She realizes the bills on the outside are HUNDREDS, but most of the bills inside are SINGLES. She's been had.

> DEL (CONT'D)
> Hey! This isn't enough! I need
> a plane tick-

She looks up. The hand is already holding a plane ticket. To London. With Del's name on it. Spooked, she just stares.

> DEL (CONT'D)
> What do you want for it?

The hand turns down, the way a hand model would display a bright shiny ring, and it wiggles its ring finger.

> DEL (CONT'D)
> You want a ring?

The hand points again, over Del's shoulder. She understands and gets to her feet.

She opens the top drawer of her night stand and carefully takes out a BEAUTIFUL DIAMOND RING.

> DEL (CON'D)
> My Dad bought this for my
> Mom in Spain. She gave it to
> me to hold onto when we left.
> Just take it. Not like it means
> anything anymore.

She admires it one last time before setting it in the palm and taking the ticket. She watches mournfully as the hand closes its fingers, then retreats back into the darkness.

Cash and ticket in hand, Del gets to her feet to pack a bag.

INT. HALLWAY - NIGHT
Del sneaks out of her room with a back pack on. She walks down the hall and heads to a nearby window, but a sound in the stairwell stops her in her tracks. Crying.

Del walks to the top of the staircase, looking down. Carla sits on the bottom steps, crying quietly to herself, head in hands. Del's face drops, and she understands what she's done.

INT. DEL'S BEDROOM - CONTINUOUS
Del drops her backpack, kneels in front of the tiny door and flings it open. In a frenzy, she unzips her back pack and dumps it on the floor. Her cash and plane ticket fall out.

> DEL
> Hey! I need my stuff back!

Del throws the cash, ticket and homework into the abyss.

> DEL (CONT'D)
> It was a mistake. I don't need
> these. I'm staying here and I
> can do my own homework.

The hand drifts calmly back out. It holds its index finger up and wags it back and forth. NO, NO, NO.

> DEL (CONT'D)
> Keep the hair, but I want my
> mom's necklace and my dad's
> ring back.

Del waits. The hand rubs its fingers together, as if deliberating. Then slowly, it makes a fist. When it opens, the ring and the necklace are there. Del grabs them, breathing a sigh of relief.

The hand, as you may have guessed, turns. GIMME, GIMME.

> DEL (CONT'D)
> No more, we're done!

The hand suddenly reaches out and snatches Del's wrist. She tries to stand and wrenches free, bolting for the door.

The arm extends, stretching impossibly long. It reaches all the way across the room, the hand becoming a taloned claw.

Just before Del reaches the door, the hand grabs her ankle, pulling her back. Del manages one quick scream before the hand yanks all the way back and through the tiny door.

It closes itself and the lock shifts quietly back into place, leaving the room still, silent, with no trace of Del. Just a mess of scattered jewelry on the floor.

FADE TO BLACK.

SHE WAS PERFECT

Cyrus could tell from across the street that Christie was perfect. Her hair was long and blonde, tight curls tied up in a messy bun on top of her head. She wore tiny white shorts that sat high up on her smooth, toned thighs and a dark green shawl that hung over her shoulders, down to her waist. Cyrus scanned up her body and saw a hint of her flat stomach under a tight-fitting tank top, the milky white skin of her chest leading up to a strong, slender neck. He wanted to run his fingers over every inch of her soft skin. Her eyes were pale blue and piercing, surrounded by lightly freckled cheeks.

They grabbed his attention, even across the four-lane street in the flurry of passing cars. He couldn't take his eyes off her. He had to talk to her. She was a show stopper, a life-changer.

He couldn't let this one get away.

From the other side of the crosswalk, Christie caught him looking. They locked eyes for only a second, but it was long enough to reveal themselves to each other. Cyrus had black hair, slicked back, with big ugly sunglasses covering most of his face. His jawline was strong and pronounced, with a subtle five o'clock shadow covering his pock-marked cheeks. His lips were pursed in an adorable permanent scowl. His dark grey slacks and black shirt weren't exactly a draw for her, but when she saw that he was watching her, she smiled. He was so serious-looking it was almost funny. But he held her attention longer than most guys did. His stoic face was oddly inviting. She wanted to know who he was.

The light changed, instructing everyone to "walk". Cyrus and Christie both shivered with an anxious flutter as they stepped into the street and walked toward each other. They stopped in the middle of the crosswalk, letting the other pedestrians pass on either side. Cyrus took off his glasses, his serious demeanor reduced to that of a nervous, bumbling teenager, as he fumbled for something to say. She let him squirm for a few seconds, holding back a laugh, but when she saw the light change to the bright red hand, she grabbed his arm and pulled him with her to the sidewalk, saving him from himself.

Cyrus couldn't believe his luck. This was the kind of girl he'd been looking for as long as he could remember, the kind of girl that would impress his family and make his friends jealous. He said the only two words that were repeating in his head, "You're… perfect."

Her face lit up with a wide smile and she said, "Good first line."

Four weeks later, Cyrus sat at a candle-lit table in the outdoor patio of an intimate and quiet restaurant, waiting for Christie to join him. He was sweating. His palms were clammy. He fidgeted with his chair, his jacket, the candles on the table, the menu, unable to hide his nervousness. Tonight was important. It would decide how the rest of his life would play out. He undid the top button of his shirt, adjusted the silverware and napkins, then redid his top button. Nothing left to fidget with, he started biting his nails. He stopped himself quickly though, he didn't want to seem too nervous when Christie arrived. He had to keep his cool, maintain composure. It was vital that he get this evening right.

To calm himself down, he went through the evening's checklist. First, he checked his jacket pocket. Of course, he'd known exactly where the tiny little box had been since the second he'd picked it up, but it was expensive, hard to find, and touching it made him feel a tiny bit better. The car was parked where it was supposed to be, the van was waiting across the street, his buddy Frankie was waiting with the camera (he'd hate to forget the photos) and arrangements had been made for the after party. So far so good. Everything was ready.

Christie parked a little further away from the restaurant than she realized. The uphill walk had coated her with a light sweat that made her thin blouse cling to her skin. Had she known there would be no valet, she would have worn different shoes. The balls of her feet were both forming blisters inside her high heels. She was already uncomfortable when she approached the restaurant and now she was dreading a long meal outside in the heat.

If she was being honest, Christie didn't want to be at this date anyway. The last date she'd had with Cyrus, he'd started making more plans before they'd gotten halfway through their meal. It was off-putting and annoying. Despite their little meet-cute on the crosswalk, she recognized that familiar, sinking feeling when he'd called last night. She'd only agreed to this date because she planned to break it off with him. And when she did, she wanted to be clear, so she would do it in person. There was no future between them. She would tell him to his face.

Cyrus saw her step around the corner and into the cozy patio. He stood up in a hurry, straightening his back to greet her, plastering a smile on his face, putting all his bright white teeth on display.

She met his big smile with a flimsy, fake one of her own and walked toward him.

"Sorry I'm a bit late. Got stuck parking over on Fifth," she said with little remorse.

Cyrus waived it off, playing it cool. "No, no, I didn't even notice."

Christie sat down and for the first time she considered the restaurant. Cyrus brought her to Murphy's Lodge, a place known for the vibe more so than the menu. She regretted coming all the way across town for shit parking and boring food, but it was too late to back out now. Her own fault for not checking the address beforehand. She settled into her chair, forcing herself to try and have a nice night before dropping a bomb on him. He had obviously taken great care in choosing this place. She felt a twinge of regret for ruining what he probably thought would be a special evening. She wasn't out to hurt his feelings, even though she probably would.

They opened up their menus. Cyrus's breaths grew shallow. A thin line of sweat formed at his hairline. She was here. It was real. Game time. He held the menu in front of him and reached into his pocket again, the little box was still there. The knot in his stomach loosened a little, and he realized that he should actually read the menu in front of him, instead of just staring at the words. She might catch on if he was too distant and suspect something was up. Couldn't have that.

The waitress arrived within a few minutes, routinely pleasant and cheerful as she took their orders. Christie ordered a salad, the fastest thing for them to prepare; while Cyrus opted for the soup, the only thing he knew he wouldn't choke on. After they ordered, Christie gave the usual vague updates on her work and her friends, normal chit chat, avoiding the real issues. Cyrus was happy to listen. The more she spoke about the trivial, everyday shit, the more time he had to mentally go through his checklist. While Christie droned on about her terrible morning commute, Cyrus absently smiled and nodded, thinking about the rest of their lives.

Christie forced every smile. Cyrus pulled every smile back about twenty percent.

During the unspectacular meal, Christie noticed that Cyrus seemed preoccupied. His mind was clearly on something else. It was unlike him, but she figured the façade of their romantic first meeting would wear off eventually, so it wasn't too surprising to see him getting distracted. He kept fidgeting, reaching into his pocket. She assumed he was bored, maybe tired from work, maybe struggling to resist checking his phone. She held onto the hope that he was over this relationship, too. That would have been a relief. But she was never that lucky.

Cyrus watched her closely, doing his best to gauge her mood. His thoughts were clouded by the box in his pocket, the van across the street. Nothing she said would impact the plan now, at least he didn't think they would. The whole thing hadn't started yet. Right now, they were having a nice, quiet dinner together. But once the evening got rolling, their lives would be thrown into a whirlwind of change. She still had no idea, and Cyrus was more anxious than ever. He had to forcefully stop his toe from tapping.

Maybe after dessert, Cyrus thought to himself while watching Christie talk. Her lips moved, her bright eyes accentuating every word with proper grace and he was again overwhelmed with how stunning she was, how luminous. Every time she moved or shifted in her chair, she looked as though she were posing for a photograph. It was effortless. And with all of her poise and beauty, he was always drawn back to her startling eyes. Those eyes could sparkle at the bottom of the sea. She was perfect. How was he so lucky to have found her?

The knot in his stomach twisted again. Almost time to fish or cut bait. But suddenly the whole thing seemed stupid. He barely knew anything about this girl. There was no way to tell what she'd do, or how she'd react. But here he was, box in his pocket, ready to take the next step with her into the future. There was still time to turn back. He could get up, walk away and forget they'd ever met. Maybe they'd both be better off. Of course, he had already told his friends back home that he'd have a show-stopping blonde with him when he returned, so it would mean facing embarrassment and shame. If he walked away now, he'd be ridiculed and forever be labeled weak. Still, maybe that was a better alternative to this plan going wrong.

The waitress dropped the "dessert or check" question and Christie jumped right in before Cyrus could say anything else. She was visibly bored now, slouched over, her elbow propped up on the table, chin resting on her hand. She thought for sure that Cyrus would call her on it. But he didn't. He had barely been listening to her talk the entire night, but he also wasn't talking much. Now, she wanted to go home and rid herself of the weird feeling she had, from this night and from Cyrus in general. Plus, she had a carton of Ben & Jerry's that she was ready to dive into once she got home, so dessert wouldn't be necessary.

"Just the check please." She flashed a lovely smile to the waitress, who nodded, and threw one back.

"You don't want dessert or coffee, or anything? I don't mind having something else," he said, stalling.

"No, I'm full and I've got something I wanted to talk to you about anyway. Away from all these people."

His stomach opened a trap door and Cyrus felt his insides hit the floor. It took everything he could muster to stop from screaming out, "Wait!"

"Something bothering you?" He forced a smile that showed too many teeth. Christie saw the strange desperation on his face and recoiled.

The waitress showed up and handed him the check. "Have a good night," she said, breaking the awkward moment. A last-ditch effort for a nice tip from the miserable couple.

Cyrus signed the check as Christie thanked him for the meal, got to her feet and threw on her coat. Cyrus stood too, sensing her urgency. He put his hand on her lower back and walked her out of the patio and onto the sidewalk.

When they were far enough from the restaurant, Christie cleared her throat and built up her courage. "Listen, I wanted to talk to you about this thing going on between us," she said softly. It was a tone meant to ease the blow. He all but ignored the comment.

"Want me to drive you to your car?"

"It's okay, we can walk and talk."

"Listen, I think I know what you're gonna say. But please, hear me out for a few minutes. I have something to say too, and I think it'll change your mind."

Christie sighed louder than she meant to and looked down the street, straining to see her car, but she couldn't. It would be a long walk back, difficult chat or not. She rolled her eyes at the idea of Cyrus trying to save their relationship, but she could at least hear him out. And if it only took him the length of the drive to her car, all the better. Then she'd have an excuse to make the dumping brief.

"Uh, yeah. Okay." Christie nodded. Cyrus motioned toward his car.

Now, he thought, *the ball is rolling.*

As she walked ahead, Cyrus checked his pocket one more time. The long slender box was, of course, right where it was supposed to be. Christie stepped toward his black Jaguar in the crowded parking lot. He unlocked the doors and quickly looked across the street to the parked white van. He nodded to its driver, then watched the blinker click on as the van merged into traffic.

Cyrus steadied himself. His palms grew sweaty as he opened the passenger door for Christie, taking care not to get in her way as she slipped into the beautiful car. As she slid into the low seat, Cyrus looked down at her thin, perfectly toned legs. They were like porcelain. A heat wave fluttered through him then, stirring up his first memory of her and he smiled to himself, knowing how lucky he was. With that image frozen in his mind, he slammed her door shut with a sense of triumph.

Looking at her through the window, he thought to himself, *Well, at least now she can't run.* He grinned at his own little joke as he walked around to the driver's side.

With the push of a button, the engine rumbled to life and Cyrus looked back into traffic, gazing on the street longer than he needed. He couldn't bring himself to look at Christie. He started to sweat again, more this time, his heart pounded, and his was mouth infinitely dry. He wouldn't fuck this up. He couldn't. He threw on his blinker, merged into traffic, and off they went, toward a new life.

Cyrus had avoided Christie's eyes for as long as possible. When he looked back at her, she'd already gotten her phone out, probably texting her friend Lilly. He figured she would likely be texting with her at some point in the evening and was suddenly worried that he hadn't factored her into his plan. Lilly, insisting that she was only acting as Christie's best friend, was always up in his business, interrogating him about who he is, what he does, where he was born and how he spends his time. She was a nuisance, and now Cyrus worried that she could throw things off, mess with his timeline. He put the thought out of his mind, for now. All he could do was focus on the task at hand and roll with whatever punches came at him.

The Jag rode smooth and steady.

"Cyrus, I really need to tell you—"

"No, no. You said you'd wait until I've said my piece," he said with a dismissiveness that Christie hated.

"Well, I've got plans with Lilly tonight, so I need to get back."

"Of course, it will only take a couple minutes."

Cyrus drove right by her car without slowing down, but she was engrossed in her text conversation and didn't notice. She was forcefully ignoring him now. Cyrus grinned to himself, inching closer and closer to the big surprise. If she didn't look up soon, he wouldn't even have to lie to her about where they were headed and what he had planned. He checked his pocket again. The box was there.

Christie was indeed texting Lilly, giving her a heads up that she'd be home earlier than expected. She didn't want to give Cyrus the idea that this should be a leisurely ride. She'd hear whatever stupid shit he had to say, then tell him it wasn't working out, step out of the car and drive home. She was so focused on looking impatient that she didn't even notice that they'd passed her street. When she finally looked up from her phone, they'd gone at least 5 blocks further than where she'd parked; her stomach lurched.

"Cyrus, you passed it. I said I'm parked back on Fifth."

"I know, but I've got a surprise for you." Cyrus had rehearsed that line and he delivered it with perfection.

Christie sighed, not caring. She had been polite, but he obviously didn't get it.

"I'm tired, Cyrus. I need to get home."

"I know, but this took me forever to set up and I think you need to see it before breaking it off with me. I promise, it won't take long."

It took everything inside of Christie to not scream in his face.

"Cyrus, come on," she said, throwing her hands up in a "what the hell" gesture. "I'm not up for whatever this is."

He'd clearly picked up on her intention of breaking it off with him and chose to ignore it. That was infuriating. But she could see that he was trying to be sweet, attempting one last romantic gesture to save them. He wasn't a bad guy, he'd misjudged her mood a bit, that's all. Plus, she could always scream at him later if this turned into a big thing.

"Make it quick, okay?"

"Quick as I can," Cyrus said through a devilish smirk.

Cyrus took the next right turn. His car glided onto a darkened, residential side street. Decorative trees dotted the sidewalks. The white van had pulled over to the curb ahead of them. The Jaguar pulled in behind it and stopped. Lights from the back of the van painted them with a dingy red glow.

Christie looked over at Cyrus, eyebrows furrowed. She was confused about what kind of surprise he had in store.

He flashed a confident smile, already pleased with himself.

This is it, this will be perfect, Cyrus thought to himself. He unbuckled his seat belt and turned his whole body to Christie. He didn't need to check his pocket again.

"I haven't known you long, Christie, but you're a lovely woman. You're smart, you're beautiful, and I think any man in the world would kill to have you."

Christie's face dropped.

No, she thought bluntly. She stopped herself from saying it out loud.

"Why are we on this street?" She started to panic when he gently took her hand in his and looked deep into her eyes, his face brimming with nervous excitement.

"I wanted us to have a moment alone in the middle of the city before both of our lives change." Another rehearsed line that hit the mark.

Cyrus reached into his pocket and he removed the box. "I have something or you."

She looked at the long rectangular box he held and breathed a small sigh of relief. It wasn't a ring box. But it looked like jewelry. She softened, her neck less tense.

"Cyrus, you shouldn't have gotten me anything." She sounded sincere. Cyrus's expression was not what she'd expect from someone giving a gift. He held his intense eye contact and squeezed her hand a little too tight. He seemed to be anticipating something, like she was about to get surprised by a hidden camera team. Shit, maybe she was. That's how ridiculous this whole thing felt.

The long black box rested in his hand, but he didn't hold it out to her. Instead, he turned her hand so her palm was facing up.

She stared down at the box, and Cyrus shook his head. "No, no, no, close your eyes."

"Cyrus, I'm trying to break up with you—" she attempted, but he stopped her.

"I know that. Close your eyes," he playfully snapped at her.

Christie clenched her jaw and closed her eyes with a loud sigh. She held her wrist up for him to latch the bracelet on. She was doing an awful lot of playing along for a gift she never asked for, and sure as shit didn't want.

Cyrus's grip tightened, and she felt a quick, sharp pinch of pressure on her forearm.

"Ow!" She yelped as her eyes shot open to see a small syringe sticking out of her arm. Faint amber liquid was plunged into her veins. She yanked her arm away, ripping open the skin. She looked up at him, unsure if this was real. It was. The needle had torn a gash in the thin skin of her wrist and the blood poured onto her beautiful dress.

"What the fuck are you doing?" She was mad, furious, too angry to be scared. But fear would soon come.

Cyrus held the same, calm smile and placed the syringe back into the long black box. Christie felt nauseous, her eyes getting heavy. Her thoughts became scattered and frantic, the connection to her physical surroundings sliding further and further away. Cyrus flashed his headlights and the rear doors of the van popped open, revealing two men ready to pounce.

In the mess that was her mind, Christie could see what was happening, but the drugs wouldn't let her feel afraid. She could only watch it unfold.

"Why did you do this?" she muttered, locking eyes with Cyrus.

Cyrus's mouth turned to a frown. He casually shrugged his shoulders like this was nothing, like he'd been asked what kind of pizza topping he liked best. He leaned close to Christie's face. The drugs kept her frozen in the front seat.

"You can't look like you do and not expect this to happen."

Her eyelids grew too heavy to keep open, and she fell deeply asleep slumped over in the front of his Jag.

Cyrus stepped out of the car and watched his boys make quick work of getting Christie into the bed of the van. They were dressed completely in black and were near impossible to spot on the poorly lit street. Any neighbors watching wouldn't be able to see how many men there were, let alone describe their faces. Once they had Christie lying on the floor, Frankie stepped in to do his part with the camera. They would hate to forget the photos. He snapped a few shots of her face, still angelic and gorgeous. Then he moved down and snapped a few pictures of her body; her strong, slender neck, the milky white skin of her chest, her flat stomach, down to her smooth, toned thighs. Cyrus was pleased, they had been totally prepared.

Frankie looked to the others and nodded, letting them know he was finished, and they launched into the next phase of the plan. They removed the false bottom of the floor and lowered Christie's unconscious body down into a coffin-like cradle they'd installed in the van's undercarriage. They secured her arms and legs with worn-down leather straps and replaced the missing piece of the van bed, completely concealing her. Nobody could see her through the windows and even if they were pulled over and searched by the cops, everything would appear normal, empty.

The van's driver stepped out and watched the professionals secure the body.

"Dammit man, how'd you land a chick like that?" He was smiling ear to ear, thoroughly impressed.

Cyrus thought before responding, "The pretty ones never see it coming."

The driver shook his head in disbelief and walked back to the wheel. Frankie hopped out of the back, holding a huge stack of thousand-dollar bills and handed it to Cyrus. He accepted it without looking and shoved it into his back pocket.

"The boss asked me to put in a little extra for this one, he liked the pictures. He wants to know how you found her." He sounded like he was a little impressed, too.

Cyrus smiled, remembering that first moment when he saw Christie across the street, and he said softly, almost to himself, "She was perfect."

Frankie shrugged and left Cyrus alone with his earnings. The back doors slammed shut, the van's engine rumbled to life and they pulled away. Cyrus tapped his back pocket, making sure the stack of money hadn't fallen out and watched as the van merged onto the busy street, disappearing into the heavy traffic, carrying Christie off to the start of her new life.

He was glad he didn't let this one get away.

PARIS WITH THE LIGHTS TURNED LOW

Everyone told Laura that she'd love Paris, that the city put beauty above everything else, but all she saw were old buildings and outdated ideas. The city frustrated her. It moved too slowly. Blood flowed differently in France. She assumed its people were full of cheese and wine. She'd grown up in hot-blooded New York City, the daughter of a hard-working painter and a commercial agent. Most of her adult life split between Manhattan and Los Angeles. In both places, millions of people did a million different things every day, with their own important agendas and frantic urgency.

That's the kind of day she liked, the pace that was most comfortable to her. But now, sitting on a slow-moving Paris metro, she tapped her feet, anxious to get back to her hotel room and get some work done. She checked her watch. It was nearing five o'clock in the evening. Her stomach rumbled, reminding her that the overnight travel and the tense meeting that afternoon had caused her to forget her lunch. Thankfully she'd only have to suffer for another fifteen minutes or so. She could handle that. It wouldn't kill her.

The train swayed gently as it turned a corner and approached the end of a dark tunnel. A handful of other passengers kept to themselves, eyes glued to phones or books. Laura looked up from the spreadsheet on her tablet just as the train burst into the daylight. Her eyes strained at the direct sun and she looked away. When her eyes relaxed a few moments later, she looked out the window again and saw a beautiful view of the Seine, flowing through the center of the city. It was mid-June, the height of tourist season, so both sides of the river were packed with people. From what she could see, it was filled with teenagers drinking bottles and bottles of wine, eating cheese or sandwiches sold in nearby shops, and sight-seers amazed with every old brick of the surrounding buildings. All of them seemed to be laughing obnoxiously. Even from this far away, that annoyed her. The decision to take the train back to her hotel, rather than walk the river, had been the right one. If she had to push through that joyous crowd, she would probably jump into the rushing water to avoid all conversation.

After a few seconds, she'd seen enough of the picturesque river. *It's beautiful, I get it,* she thought. Laura looked back to her iPad, trying to refocus on the business at hand. The company's first international acquisition was in the works, but they all knew it would be a delicate process. As the new CFO, the pressure would be squarely on her to make it happen. She needed every bit of brainpower to comb through the mountain of numbers, legal jargon, and the inflated, bullshit yearly budget that had been submitted to her. But everyone back in LA trusted her to handle it, and she would. She could get hit with curve balls all day. She wouldn't be distracted from her goal.

The company, Visual Extremes, handled advertising for movie studios and TV networks, which is a tough market to break into and even tougher to maintain. But Laura had worked hard since her early twenties, fostering relationships she'd made as an assistant. She was known for being a bull. Once she set her sights on something, there was little you could do to stop her from getting it. People liked that about her until they found themselves in her crosshairs.

She managed to get her tiny foot in the big door of Hollywood by impressing the famous producer, Michael

Linder, brother of mega star Wallace Linder. On the strength of her own hard work, she'd been able to snatch clients out from under them, despite their own stellar reputations and a famous name. Laura was shocked when Michael called her directly to say that he was impressed. A few weeks later, after several lunches together, he asked her to combine her tenacity with his company's experience and clout and together build a company that could outlive them both.

Laura questioned his offer for only a few minutes. When she convinced herself that Michael wasn't trying to screw her or bury her, she happily shook his hand and brought a handful of young, up and coming producers into the company with her. She worked her ass off for nearly a decade and she was elated that somebody of Michael's status had noticed and embraced her. She was the new CFO of a company with history and prestige, doing work that she loved and she had more respect for Michael than she thought she would have for anyone. And he trusted her enough to send her to Paris and secure the acquisition of the French advertising company Lumière Rageuse, which meant Raging Light.

The first thing to go will be that stupid name, she'd thought the first time she'd heard it.

Laura found the small French company a year before when an editor friend worked with them before landing a couple of features and moving on. But he'd sent her a few of their online projects and she realized the small team had a great handle on the European audience, which her own team had yet to really crack. Her first act as CFO was convincing Michael to purchase the Parisian boutique. He didn't hesitate for a second before agreeing. He'd sent her to Paris with a blank check and an order not to leave without a deal. The pressure was squarely on her, which was how she liked it.

Before she hopped on the train, Laura was at a meeting with the top men at the company, which went surprisingly well, despite their clear and open disdain for her. The sour face of the receptionist that greeted her should have been a clue as to how the meeting would begin, but she was still surprised at how outwardly rude these Frenchmen were. Marcel Bernard, the eldest was clearly in charge. He didn't smile, didn't look her in the eye, didn't stand to greet her or shake her hand. The other men did greet her, but she could tell from their half-hearted mutterings of "Bonjour" or "Bienvenue", that the rest of the men were his lackies. They would stare at their own feet until Marcel spoke. But Laura wasn't worried, she'd dealt with her fair share of assholes in the business world. Misogyny was simple, easy to manage. Some men didn't like her, didn't want to deal with her. In fact, their rudeness put her more at ease, more in control of the situation. She wouldn't feel so bad throwing her weight around in the negotiations, stomping out a few more of their requests and calling out a few more lines in the budget that she knew were bullshit.

While they'd tried to show their dislike of her with vague, non-descript whining, she figured out about within the first few minutes why they were giving her such a hassle. Three times, they asked her to get Michael Linder on the phone to get his opinion on something. Twice, she politely refused with, "I'm sorry, Mr. Linder is busy this afternoon, but he's put his full confidence in me, so I can answer any questions you may have."

The third time, she sharpened her claws. Instead of politeness, she shot back, "Mr. Linder is unavailable to you, sirs. Now if you'd like to move forward with this acquisition, you deal with me." She reminded them that Michael was on urgent business with Warner Brothers, and that superseded the petty requests of Lumière Rageuse. She made sure to pronounce their ridiculous name perfectly. "And after the deal goes through, it will be me you continue to speak with."

That stopped their whining.

She flashed them all a smile. Marcel left the room, scoffing and shaking his head, jiggling the fat under his chin. Two of his partners followed him like lemmings. She watched Marcel through the glass door, yelling at his people, waving his fist pointing back at the conference room. Laura's smile was bulletproof. The other Frenchmen sat in the uncomfortable silence with her, none of them meeting her eye, until Marcel stepped back into the room, calmer. He shot back a shit-eating smile of his own.

"Oui, I understand, Mademoiselle. A simple miscommunication. Shall we continue?"

The rest of the meeting flew by with little resistance. Neither side pushed back against objections, the conversation was productive, even pleasant at times. The more that was agreed upon, the better Laura felt about the whole deal. She'd ruffled feathers a bit more than she meant to, but that's how business was done in the States. Laura would have to warn Michael that the personalities might be an obstacle, but nothing she couldn't handle. All in all, despite her complete and utter lack of interest in the city itself, the trip was going well.

At the end of the meeting, Marcel insisted they all have a celebratory drink to toast the forging of a successful partnership. Laura didn't want a drink. There was nothing to celebrate yet, but the proposal was good and she didn't know a polite way to refuse the gesture. The assistants brought in drinks on silver trays; scotch for the men, sherry for her. Laura sighed to herself. She'd just let that one go for now. She threw back her tiny drink, and everyone cheered.

Laura clicked off the iPad in her lap and leaned back

in her seat on the train. Her eyes started to feel heavy. The gentle rocking of the train, the jet lag, the exhaustive meeting and the shockingly strong sherry were all working together to put her to sleep. Her hotel bed sounded like Heaven on Earth. With her eyes closed, she felt her insides lurch, the liquid in her stomach sloshing side to side. Her hand moved from rubbing her eyes to her belly as a wave of cold cramping nausea swept through her. She was sure she was going to vomit. Her chest heaved as she breathed deeply, trying to control her insides and keep from spewing all over the metro. Her bathroom suddenly looked as good as her bed.

She clenched a fist, crumpling the bottom of her blouse, and focused hard on keeping her food down (or up, depending on which way it chose to flee). After about 30 seconds, the chilly ache subsided. She didn't think it was motion sickness. It might be her period coming early, but most likely it was a bit of gas. She breathed a sigh of relief as the dull pain retreated deeper into her body and warmed into nothing. Her skin felt damp. The shrieking metal on metal of the brakes drilled into Laura's head as the train slowed toward the next station. The lights in the car flickered as she forced her eyes open to check the station sign. The last thing she wanted to do was miss her stop.

She was at Maubert Mutualite. Her hotel was off the Jussieu station. Two more stops. Her plan was to get off at her station and grab a bite to eat on the walk and spend the rest of the evening plugging away on her laptop in the room. But now, in the sensitive state her stomach was in, she thought she'd plop herself onto the bed, suffer through a room service call of half broken English and half lazy French. At least she'd be off her feet. Even sitting on the metro was proving difficult. One more deep breath secured the contents of her stomach as the doors of the metro hissed closed. No one had gotten on or off. This stop was all but abandoned.

Laura's queasiness was replaced by dizziness as the train started to move again, but even after it got up to speed and the ride smoothed out, her head was still swimmy. She slid her iPad into her bag so as not to drop it and smash it to pieces on the unforgiving floor. She steadied herself, closing her eyes again, and tried to regain her balance. Her brain felt like liquid, her thoughts bounced around like bubbles in a whirlpool. Opening her eyes made it worse. She gripped the handrail near her seat, braced herself against the swaying car, clenched her jaw, and squeezed her eyelids closed.

Something was wrong. Her mind started its frantic search for a way to protect her, running through everything she'd eaten so far to locate the source of her sudden pain. Her day started with a Starbucks yogurt from the airport. Should be no problem there, that was a usual start to her mornings. She'd gotten an espresso and a Danish-like pastry from a little café outside the Lumière Rageuse offices, and despite the massive amount of butter they'd used, those both seemed harmless. She'd had a single piece of heavy blue cheese wrapped in a thin prosciutto during the meeting, only to be polite. Delicious as it was, she doubted it would wreak havoc on her insides. And that was it.

The thought crossed her mind that she was overly hungry, she hadn't had a full meal since landing and she was probably a little tired from the trip and the meeting. But no, that wasn't it. This didn't feel like usual hunger, that lack of energy that forces you to shut down. This was something actively wrong inside of her, forcing her into this strange state. Maybe the filthy train had given her a bug, a parasite, leeching itself onto her brain stem and pulling energy from her. That was a bit ridiculous of course, but given what she was feeling, Laura didn't want to rule out something like that.

Her eyes shot open excitedly as the train slowed, and she checked the sign again. Not her stop. She was at Gare d'Austerlitz station, One stop away from the one she wanted. She was half relieved to not have to stand and walk at the moment, but half worried about what would happen if she sat on the train for much longer.

As the car rolled to a loud stop, she realized this station was far busier than the previous. The map showed the station had two lines overlapping, which meant hundreds of people coming and going with every train. Sure enough, the door hissed open, and a flood of passengers pushed and shoved their way into her space. At least she had a seat. She kept her head down while people settled in place for the ride. She wanted to ignore them, suffer alone. Thankfully, that's what they all wanted, too. Eyes to the floor, she fought the encroaching dizziness that was taking over.

One more stop. One more, then you can lie down. This will pass.

The car's lurch forward brought a new wave of nausea. She couldn't tell if it was the same raw feeling in her stomach or if the motion of the train was shifting her insides around, but either way, she was miserable. Looking out the window, Laura squinted at the people left in the station trying to see their faces in the dark cavernous station.

She was starting to panic. Nothing she felt was familiar. Thoughts blended together in one single stream, a series of visions looking into her body, desperate to find what could possibly be causing her illness, so sudden and extreme. Her stomach had never turned the way it was turning now, she'd never had a dizzy spell that lasted more than a few seconds (or a couple minutes, if you included the occasional ground shake in LA). The panic she felt intensified the foreign feelings in her body. She shivered, a wave of ice spreading out from her spine.

All at once, she was certain she couldn't stay conscious for the trip. Her stop might as well be six hours away. Her eyelids grew heavy. She scooted her butt to the back of her seat and doubled over, not caring that her shoulders brushed against a stranger's legs. Sweat beaded on her forehead. She needed to get off the damn metro.

Laura looked to her left and met the eyes of an elderly man in a grey overcoat across the aisle, one of the many passengers she hadn't noticed before. She opened her mouth to speak. The effort she put forth did nothing more than pull her dry lips apart. She felt them slowly separate, as though they'd been stuck together for hours. Her face was numb. A creaky sliver of breath forced its way out of her tightening throat, getting nobody's attention but her own.

A seizure, she thought, but could not express. Her eyes drifted down to her hands. She made a fist with her right hand; fingers opened and closed, opened and closed. She tried her left. Same thing. She still had control of her body. All was right in the world of arms and legs, but her mind was sinking deeper and deeper into an unseen abyss.

The train burst into daylight again, but darkness crept in around the edges of her sight, her peripheral vision faded slowly away like an old film print. She looked up again to find the old man in the grey overcoat, mustered every bit of strength she could, and from the bottom of her diaphragm, she yelled, but what came out was nothing above a normal "Hey."

"Pardon?" He said in a thick French accent. He stared at her blankly, watched as she tried to speak, but she was at odds with her own body. Her suit jacket was off and jammed in the seat beside her, her skirt pulled up a little too far, her hair looked great earlier in the day but was now a tussled mess, and she was sweating, giving her ebony skin a shine that she was sure everyone on the train would notice. She must have looked drunk.

"Huuuulllppppp," she muttered through nearly closed lips.

Even if she'd been able to shout "Help" clearly, the old man may not know a word of English, because he turned away and ignored her, shaking his head disapprovingly.

Without any warning, Laura puked. Her nausea evolved into full-fledged evacuation. The hot mess of food, coffee and bile shot up with a gassy, flooding sound from her throat. She spewed the brown and green liquid out in front of her, decorating pant legs and shoes of the poor souls (and soles) near the door. The passengers, who silently complained about having to ride on such a crowded train with their elbows tucked in and shoulders hunched, suddenly found space to jump back and away from the horrid-smelling vomit.

Laura's cries for help went unfinished, dying behind

her teeth as she fell forward and landed with her hands in the splatter of puke. Her eyes did the screaming for her. Her thoughts competed between finding someone to get her to a hospital and finding the reason for the growing pain in her stomach and head.

People retreated in disgust, yelling "Ivrogne!" as they scowled. The train came to a stop, the doors hissed open, and the stampede plowed out the doors in record time.

With the doors frozen open for a few moments, Laura knew she couldn't let them close with her still inside. She pulled one hand out of the nasty puddle and grabbed the side of her seat. With her lunch oozing through her fingers, she managed to pull her torso upright resting on her knees.

A second was all she had to rest as the familiar ding signaled that the doors were about to close. Adrenaline helped get one stiletto under her body and she rose up to a standing position, finding her center by wobbling.

New passengers piled in around her, none of them aware of the horrid smell they were about to be locked in with. A few of them bumped Laura's shoulders, nearly knocking her over again, but there were plenty of poles, railings and innocent bystanders for her to grab hold of, so she managed to stay upright.

The doors glided closed as Laura threw herself forward. She grabbed the rubber bumpers and pushed her body between them, escaping the train with not a second to spare. Safely on the platform, she remembered her briefcase was still on the train. She looked back, but the turn of her head made her feel even more woozy and she lost any ounce of concern for her tablet and her laptop. All she could do was find a way a hospital or to someone who could help.

"Hhhhhuuuullllllmmmm," she muttered to herself, barely audible.

Her stomach felt like it had been scraped out with an old spoon. At the same time, she felt hungry, but sure she could hold nothing down. Her head, not only dizzy, pounded in her skull, pushing angrily against the back of her eyes. Her tongue swelled. Bumps like canker sores rose up within minutes of each other.

In the chaotic storm of thoughts that blew through her mind, one word shot out and stayed clear in her head, like a group of red 7s hitting their mark on a lucky slot machine. In big red letters, she saw: POISON.

Her next thoughts focused on that single idea. She thought through her day again, *when did I take poison?* But right then, it didn't matter. She needed to get off this platform. Her steps were unstable, her knees shook and nearly buckled with each step. Her muscles grew weak and she was sure that within a matter of minutes, she'd be completely paralyzed. It'd be better if she were above-ground when it happened.

The stairs wouldn't even give her pause on a usual day. She was a gym rat when she had the time, but now the flight of stairs looked like a straight shot into the sky, ten stories, at least, though it was really only one. Laura gripped the handrail as tightly as she could and pulled herself up, every step slow and careful. Metal scraped as the old handrail pulled away from the wall, the old rusty screws working hard. It was another stinging reminder of this run-down city. Her disdain for it bubbled up again. She was pissed that her life was now in the hands of Paris and if everything was going to fall apart on her like this fucking handrail, she wouldn't make it out alive.

Anxious passengers pushed by her on the stairs, all hurrying to their destinations. She let them pass and pulled herself up, one painful step at a time. She looked drunk, sounded drunk, and after vomiting, she smelled drunk, too. Weakness in her muscles was not a lack of strength, but an opposing force, slowly dissembling her limbs, thread by thread allowing less and less force with every pull. She would fight it for as long as she could. Laura Walton would never let weakness be the end of her.

She expected her eyes to hurt from the bright sunlight as she neared the top of the staircase. Instead, it seemed dark outside. It was only around 6pm. Summertime in Paris, the sun doesn't set until 10pm, so it should have been sunny and beautiful. Confused, she planted a foot on the sidewalk, ground level, and looked around, trying to get a sense of her surroundings. She expected to feel the cool air, hear the loud sounds of traffic, smell the gasoline from passing cars and ferries on the river below. But her nose felt congested, her skin thick and numb, her ears clogged. Around her, hundreds of people went about their day. Many of them had sunglasses on, squinting in the bright sun, so the darkness outside was hers and hers alone. Her senses were failing. Her eyes were joining in the descent toward the endless dark.

Laura marched forward. She didn't know where she was or which direction to move, but her instinct brought her toward the street. Rather than chance the crosswalk – it seemed like the drivers didn't pay much attention to them anyway – Laura stopped herself, leaning on a surprisingly fancy trashcan. With a momentary rest, she felt okay, all things considered. The dizziness had given way to something beneath it; a dull, dim nothing that lurked beneath her consciousness, creeping up to take over her mind entirely.

Is this how people die? she thought to herself. *Will they find me dead with no explanation?*

Usually, Laura didn't end up anywhere she didn't want to be. Paris was the one exception. The one time she'd allowed other people to dictate her decisions. Michael Linder was a magic worker when it came to getting people to do his bidding, and she bit. Big time. Look where it got her. The city around her was held up to heaven-like status by all the world, but all she saw was old things. She felt crazy amid her slow, quiet decent. The only person who didn't like Paris would find her death under the fucking Notre Dame. Perfect.

Her hope waning, her will slowly dripping from her like sweat, she again thought through everything she'd had. There had to be something she was missing. The espresso, the cheese, the celebratory drink, the-

She stopped. Another slot machine moment hit. The sherry in the office. That smile that Marcel had flashed while handing her the glass. The insistence to have a drink and "seal the deal". That was it. Those bastards at Lumière Rageuse had given her that drink. She was the only one with sherry. It was the only thing that made any kind of sense. They wanted her out of the way, out of their hair. They wanted to deal with Michael, they made that clear. She told them they couldn't, that they'd have to go through her. Maybe it was lost in translation, but that's exactly what those bastards were doing. They were going right through her.

The revelation brought up what was left in her stomach. Laura puked again, this time into the decorative trash can. Passersby gasped and moved away in disgust, but she ignored them. They didn't matter. She stayed hunched over, heaving and heaving until it was all out of her. Her lips were dry and cracking now. She was crying. Green and yellow vomit dripped from her bottom lip. When she was certain she was done for at least a few minutes, she pulled her head out of the fancy trash and steadied herself. Her eyes settled on the darkening city, the distant buildings shifting in and out of focus. What could she do? What was left? There was no way to know how much time she had left. Based on the rapid progression of her body's shutdown, she'd guess only a half-hour or so. Not enough time. Unless…

No, she thought, defiantly. She was still breathing, still conscious, and still able to think. While she had those things, she would work toward surviving. But it was more than survival that lit the fire under her. She wanted revenge. Those smarmy French fucks thought they could do something this vile, this horrifically cruel and things would fall into place, the way they wanted them. Her life wasn't important, didn't need to be factored in or considered with any of their plans. Well, Laura had spent the last fifteen years dealing with men who thought that way. And she'd bested them all, left them behind on her climb to better things, leaving them groveling and complaining, trying to figure out how this bitch had gotten ahead of them. So, she had a few minutes left? She'd use them to fuck these guys.

With a revitalized strength of purpose, Laura weighed

her options. Hospital seemed the smartest plan. Save herself, live to fight another day. But what if she didn't make it? She'd die on the street, or in the back of a cab. People would eventually realize that she'd been poisoned, but that could take weeks and she doubted they'd suspect a bunch of film people. Her phone could have helped, but of course that was travelling East, probably sliding around in a thinning puddle of her stomach contents. Her words failed her, they would be of no use in English, anyway. And if she didn't start moving now, her legs would be useless, too. The idea that she landed on, while not the best option, was the only one that yielded any path to justice.

Laura would walk back, march into the Lumière Rageuse office and die on the floor of that fucking conference room. That would raise a few questions, in whatever language they liked. They'd find poison in her system and she assumed they'd find evidence of the same poison in the offices. If not, they'd at least consider the shady men running the place. That was her best shot at winning this one. Collapsing on the floor of their tacky red offices gave her the chance to see the look on their stupid faces when they realized that she'd figured it out and was able to get the best of them anyway. She could die after seeing that.

Leaving the stable trash can, she threw herself forward, forcing her feet to either act or let her fall.

Thankfully they fell in line and her legs followed suit, carrying her toward the concrete staircase at the end of the sidewalk. Rather than taking a chance crossing the street, she stumbled toward a staircase, leading down to the river walk. There, she'd have a direct line back to the offices, which she remembered where right next to the water. If she could stagger along the riverside, she'd be able to find the right building. The Frenchmen had made a big show, trying to impress her with their new patio over-looking the river. All she'd have to look for were colored lights and the incredibly tacky tiki bar set up on their fifth floor. She hoped she'd be able to tell them that their tasteless indulgence was one of the things that screwed them.

Steps had become a worthy adversary, but she managed, and her heels clopped down onto the flat surface of the riverside walkway. The helpful momentum of gravity was gone, in its place was left an added difficulty of navigating the crowd. The riverside was wide, at least thirty feet from the water to the high stone wall, but it was packed with people. Joggers out en masse, kids and adults alike swooping by on roller blades dodging pedestrians with expert level precision, and all the loud, drunk, obnoxious teenagers that Laura had spotted from the train.

She kept her eyes straight ahead, narrowing her sight to only the people in her direct path. Breathing heavily through her nose like a charging bull, she didn't worry about bumping shoulders, spilling peoples' drinks, or the ice-cold side-eye from angry people as she pushed her way through them.

She dragged her feet, jaw hanging, eyelids fluttering. She did her damndest to keep her eyes open, despite the invisible 10-pound weight tied to them. Laura's throat had begun to weaken too, and without realizing it, she was letting out a soft, deep moan with every painful exhale. That turned a few heads but wouldn't elicit anything more than a grunt of disapproval.

She pushed and pushed, keeping her focus as much as she could. It was working. Her legs were like a machine and the river walk continued to whoosh by her in a flurry of activity. She felt strong pins and needles in her left hand and forearm, slowly climbing her arm, toward her heart. Her tongue throbbed, more white bumps formed on the top. But on she pushed, eyes blurred, throat cracked and closing, nerves failing in her limbs, every step threatening to become her last.

A full mile behind her, Laura moved fast. Sheer determination lit the fire under her and kept her legs pumping like pistons. The furious pace of her march slowed the effects of the poison, but the persistent mixture was working its way deeper into her system. It burrowed into her brain, pulling her senses further and further from clarity, making it harder for her thoughts to stay together in her head. It coursed through her veins and into her heart, leaving more and more of itself stuck inside the chambers of the pounding muscle, slowing it down, making every beat a fraction weaker than the last. And it continued shutting down her sight, further dimming the lights over Paris.

Laura spent the energy to look up briefly, putting her eyes into the direct sunlight. It didn't hurt. Instead, the sky looked dark brown, the sun itself a yellowish circle pasted onto it. The daylight was like she'd never seen. She wondered if anyone had seen a sky like the one she saw. A sudden twinge of sadness came forward when she realized that she would be dead before she could tell her father, an avid painter of landscapes and skies, about what her failing eyes had shown her.

Her eyes gave her a final gift before they parted ways. She saw the building and those stupid fucking colored lights strung across the patio, connecting the faux bamboo tiki bar to the ultra-modern sliding glass doors.

Her gamble paid off. Her vengeance was within reach.

The excitement of seeing the building caused her fragile focus to wander long enough to throw off her balance. Her next step was the slightest bit off center and her knee buckled. Her arms flailed upward, her addled body tried to keep itself from toppling over, but failed.

She fell forward. Her face hit first, taking most of the weight of her body. She felt her cheek bone splinter under her skin. Her right eye immediately filled with blood. Pedestrians on the street backed away at the brutal fall while Laura lay on the ground with her mangled cheek pressed against the hot concrete.

All at once, Laura felt the poison take hold. She sucked in as much air as she could with an alarming wheeze that told her that her lungs were the next to go on strike. Her arms wouldn't move, they only spasmed when she tried. Her legs brought her as far as they could, like a horse that marched until its heart gave out, giving one last step after death.

There would be no vengeful death, no satisfying terror in her killers' eyes. Her dead, twisted body would be left on the sidewalk for all these assholes to see. They'd wonder about her, ask each other if they knew what happened to that random black woman who died by the river.

Back home, they'd hear about how she died and wonder for the rest of their lives what happened. She thought about her father weeping in his room, her brother and sister trying to explain her death to their kids, thought about her dog adjusting to a new owner. Laura let all the sadness flood her fractured thoughts. She figured there were only a handful conscious seconds before she was swept away by the dark cloud surrounding her. For the first time in her life, there was no more fight left in her.

Dozens of feet surrounded her, most of them in bright-colored sneakers, a few high heels, and one very nice pair of loafers. She felt a couple of hands on her, gently shaking her shoulders to see if she was awake. All it did was grind her busted cheek into the ground. With her eyes rolling back in her head, Laura heard one voice echo in the distance; a kid, from the sound of it, no older than fifteen.

"Madame? Quel est le problème?"

She focused every ounce of her falling energy into one action. One by one, she consciously pulled energy from her feet, her legs, her hips, her intestines, her liver, her stomach, her spine, her neck, and finally, she closed her eyes. Her lungs sucked in one last shallow gasp of air, her lips and her tongue shaped one word in her mouth.

Weak and pitiful, she pulled everything she had to whisper the word, "Poison."

Without knowing whether or not it was understood, Laura slipped away into unconsciousness. The city darkened to a total black, and all her thoughts dissolved into nothingness.

★★★

She'd been missing for two weeks. The story went mostly unnoticed, buried deep in the news, telling of a drunk woman stumbling through crowds along the Siene, who then had a scary fall, injuring herself. Nothing about poison, nothing about her being American, or her being in town on to meet with local businessmen. The Frenchmen didn't have a good answer for what happened to her. They assumed because she hadn't been heard from since their meeting, that she'd succumbed to the poison they'd put in her sherry – a move they now thought was genius – and died alone somewhere, out of sight. Maybe she'd fallen into the river and she'd been carried to the sea. That was the best case scenario.

The reporters didn't write that her briefcase had been found in a puddle of dried vomit on a metro car. When the cops realized that the expensive-looking leather case didn't house a bomb and that some poor distracted businessperson had simply forgotten their briefcase, they went to work finding who it belonged to. Inside, they found an American passport for Laura Walton from New York City. The Frenchmen remained blissfully unaware that the cops were able to match it to the drunk woman found near the river.

Satisfied with the outcome of their poisonous little scheme, the Frenchmen had set up a new meeting, feigning anger and annoyance at the delay caused by Laura's disappearance. Michael Linder, in turn, had decided to go to Paris himself, to smooth things over and make sure they knew how dedicated Visual Extremes was to the acquisition.

Michael was devastated to hear that Laura had gone missing while abroad, and when he conferred with the Paris Police department, he'd had to stop himself from blubbering with worry and concern. As they talked him through everything they knew – her odd scene by the river, the discovery of her briefcase, her ominous final word to the teens – he made it clear to the police that Laura was important to him and he would do whatever he could to help find out what happened.

So, when the calls came in from Lumière Rageuse, sounding irritated and petty, obviously trying to use the tragic situation to their own advantage, he decided that he would handle the new negotiations himself, to see these pricks in person.

Michael Linder arrived in Paris alone. He didn't have the usual crew of assistants behind him, carrying two phones each, keeping his life in order. Unlike Laura, he absolutely adored Paris. But this trip wasn't about seeing artwork at Musèe d'Orsay or eating pain au chocolat from his favorite bakery. This was business he had to get right.

An aging police officer, Reno, stubbornly holding onto every bit of 80s style he could, met him at the airport with a car waiting outside. He shook Reno's hand, squeezing it too hard in his anxiety. They'd spoken on the phone twice, the first time for the police to inquire about the missing woman's presence in Paris, the other to explain what they thought may have happened, a theory that brought Michael into Charles De Gaulle airport.

"It is as we suspected, Monsiuer Linder," Reno confirmed with a nod, moustache dancing under his nose.

Michael nodded, understanding. "I'm glad to hear it. None of this was easy for us to swallow," Michael said.

"We will have it all sorted soon. You are going straight to the appointment, I presume?" Michael nodded. "Good. I will drive you myself. My colleagues will meet us there."

Reno led Michael to an unmarked police car, and they drove through the busy streets of downtown Paris. Michael could barely say a word. He'd insisted on having the meeting with Marcel and his panel of goons as soon as he stepped off the plane, he considered having the men from Lumière Rageuse meet him at the airport, but this was going to be delicate. It wasn't going to be a negotiation. It was a power move. He needed this meeting to go exactly as planned.

Reno dropped him off in front of the Lumière Rageuse building. Michael announced himself to the receptionist. They'd been expecting him, of course, so he didn't have to sit on the lobby's hideous red leather couch.

Those will be the first things to go when I take over. Well, second, after changing the stupid name, he thought.

A tightly wound businessman walked into the lobby, hand extended to shake before he was even through the door. He was obviously sent in by Marcel with instructions to be cheerful and welcoming.

"Ah, bonjour Monsiuer Linder. T'ank you for making 'de trip to Paree. We are excited to meet wit' yeu." His accent was so exaggerated it seemed offensive.

"Very glad to be here, although I wish it was under happier circumstances. I was truly looking forward to having Laura in charge of the Parisian arm of our business."

"Oui, oui. She seem eh, very capable, very charming. We hope she is found soon."

Michael smiled wide, showing as many teeth as he could. He marveled to himself at how brazen this man was, how confident, how simple it was for him to lie about his dear friend Laura.

"How about we get on with this? Smooth everything over, yes?" Michael said through his forced grin.

Thinking that was the last of their worries, the businessman nodded emphatically and led Michael through the hallways, talking his ear off about the remodel they'd done, bringing the offices into the modern age of Paris.

"You must see our new patio tiki bar," the businessman said.

Michael heard none of it. He walked behind, texting Reno, the meeting was about to happen. He was ready. The plan was a go.

Michael stepped into the oversized conference room that Laura had walked into only two weeks before, and he immediately took control. He leaned forward on the desk and made eye contact with each nervous underling sitting around the fat old man at the other end of the table, Marcel. "Okay everyone, let's do away with pleasantries. Nobody wants to be here right now. Before we get started negotiating this deal, I have a question for the room." He let the suspense linger for a moment. "Why is it that people want to do business with me?"

The Frenchmen exchanged a few glances. Marcel shot daggers at him, thinking he was about to deal with another American cowboy who thought they knew best. The room was quiet for fifteen uncomfortable seconds. This was a surprising, unexpected opening line, but someone had to answer.

The bravest of them, the man who had walked in with Michael, took a swing, "Because you are the best."

"Wrong," Michael countered, immediately. "I am,

but why?"

Another hero: "Because you've got the experience."

"I do, but no." Michael's phone buzzed in his pocket. A text from Reno: *30 seconds.*

"Anyone else?"

Marcel, in an attempt to regain a little of the composure his team had lost, grumbled from his chair, not hiding his annoyance with Michael. "Because you know what you want."

Michael snapped and pointed a finger at the old man, showing them all that he was correct.

"And when I know what I want, you know what happens?" He wasn't waiting for the guesses this time. "I fucking get it."

Outside the room, there was a small commotion. More people came into the office from outside.

"I told you all that I want Laura Walton to oversee this merger. So guess what..."

The door to the conference room pushed open and Reno walked in, pushing a wheelchair. A confused and terrified assistant followed him in a half-assed attempt to stop him. In the wheelchair, sat Laura Walton. Some of the men gasped, some of them froze solid, but they were all stunned.

Laura had begun a long recovery from the poisoning – arsenic, they'd discovered – but the brain damage had left her nearly blind. Her arms and legs might come back to life with intensive physical therapy, but her days as a gym rat were over. Her eyes had gone from beautiful brown to glassy silver/grey, and they darted around the room, grabbing any light they could, finding the terrified expressions on the Frenchmen's' faces. Satisfied, she laughed, savoring this moment.

"Bonjour," Laura managed with a crooked grin.

Reno studied their reactions carefully as some of them shouted objections to Laura being in the room, like they couldn't make sense of it in their own minds and just had to resist however they could. They'd already written her off as dead.

In that moment, the only sense they could make of her was that she must be a demon, back from the dead to eat them alive.

That wasn't totally wrong.

Laura smiled, only one half of her mouth going the distance, and spoke confidently.

"Okay, where were we?"

MUSIC FROM THE GUN ROOM

I've never known quite how to feel about the night I recorded with *The Kicks*. I was only seventeen, so the idea of laying down our own stuff was still new and exciting. But I had no idea how hard it would be, or how much that night would impact the lives of everyone involved. Nobody left that session unscathed. And after twenty years of thinking about it, the memory brings both a smile to my face and a cold sweat to my palms. So, when my ten-year-old son walked up and handed me the scratched-up silver CD, my heart skipped a beat and I gasped.

"Dad," Danny said, "can you play this or what?"

I looked again at the disc he'd found buried in some

dusty old box or another. The only thing written on it was *The Kicks, 2002*, scribbled on the top with a thick black Sharpie. Danny was just becoming interested in music, absorbing everything in every genre he could find. I should have guessed he'd go snooping around my old CDs at some point.

He stared at me with wide, hopeful eyes, excited to hear a yes. But I hesitated, struggling to decide whether I wanted him to know about *The Kicks* or not. It had been private for so long that I was stunned into silence, a statue of indecision.

"Where'd you find this," I asked, bewildered.

"It was wedged in your high school yearbook. Did you make this?"

I nodded, absently. Before I give him an answer, before I let my young son in on the joy and the nightmare of that night, I get lost in the memory.

★★★

The four of us had agreed to record everything we had in one night. We thought that would be spontaneous and cool, but really it meant that we were unprepared for everything. Elliot Voss and I were the optimists, as usual. We figured it would be easy, since it was all stuff we'd played before and it was only six songs to get through. Derek Ouellette and Jesse Alan didn't think we could do it at all. To be fair, with no money to spend, renting amps and mixers was out of the question. And asking any of our parents for help would be a joke, so we'd have to figure out some logistics, for sure. But after wearing them down for a week, we convinced the two pessimists that we should give it a shot.

After school that Friday, half the band went out to scrape together enough cash for extra guitar strings and drum sticks, while Elliot and I were in search of gear. This was Southern Maine in 2002, so iPhones and digital recorders were still the thing of dreams. Other high school bands still had old cassette recorders they used to lay down their songs - mostly punk bands who weirdly didn't care that no one could understand their vocals - but if we wanted a proper album, we'd need to find some proper equipment.

We ended up in the living room of a senior girl named Steph Bergeron. She was an upper-classman, arguably the hottest girl in the entire school. But her father had given her a brand-new amp head and mixer for her to record herself singing for auditions, so there we stood. We trembled at the sight of her wavy red hair and worked hard to not look straight down her thin, loose-fitting sweater every time she bent over. We had to focus on the task at hand.

Standing beside me, Elliot shifted from side to side, tugging at the bottom of his black Champion sweater, while I ran my hands through my long black hair too many times. Both of us tapped our feet, fidgeting while she glared back, arms crossed in front her.

"You know I literally got these like yesterday? I haven't even used them yet." She was annoyed we were even asking.

"So, it's still in the box," I said. "Safer for us to haul back and forth."

She rolled her eyes. Her arms crossed tighter, exposing a bit more cleavage, and she squinted as she looked me up and down, sizing me up before making her decision. She looked a little concerned about my faded and ripped jeans but her scrunched up expression told me that she was downright worried about the pentagram on my Godsmack t-shirt.

"This rig is my baby and I'm supposed to record with it next week."

Elliot and I nodded along as she listed all the reasons she shouldn't let us use it. She was clearly right to be nervous. Our band consisted of four teenage boys, historically known to be the least responsible type of human, so her caution was well-placed. We couldn't begrudge her that. But, Steph liked our stuff. She'd seen us play a couple songs in the talent show the year before and to our genuine surprise, she had showered us with compliments after our set, comparing us to a handful of 70s bands that she loved like Zeppelin and Sabbath. So naturally, we were hoping she'd help her fellow musicians in our time of need.

Sure enough, once her well of excuses ran dry, she put

her hands on her hips, let out a huge sigh– "You can use them, but make sure that every single person there is aware that these are mine, that they're very expensive, and if anything happens to them, I will kill every one of you."

"Got it," we said almost in unison.

"I'm so serious, Simon," she raised a finger and pointed it right at my nose, "If I find one scratch on the top of this, I will eat your balls for lunch, got it?"

I assumed she was kidding, though I figured there was an outside chance she'd do just that if we fucked it up. Either way I got the message. She was going to help us out, but she would remain in a state of panic until we brought it all back.

"It will come back in better shape than you gave it. This is huge. We owe you one, Steph," I said, trying to stay cool. I was honestly touched that such a badass, older girl was willing to help out a few scrawny sophomores.

I had an obvious crush on Steph, there was no hiding that. I'm sure she knew it too, but neither of us would ever say that out loud. I should admit though, after she said yes, I fantasized about returning the equipment to her front door, sitting in her basement listening to our newly minted record, studying her reaction as she bobbed her head to the beat, then making out with her for hours.

Elliot and I followed her into the back room. The head and the mixer were indeed still in the boxes, sitting neatly in the corner of the family's music room. I felt a twinge of jealously seeing such a well-equipped music room, but ultimately it didn't matter, because we were going to record a fucking rock and roll CD thanks to Steph. The music we'd been working on for months would finally get out into the world. The idea of recording filled me with delusions of grandeur, visions of our scribbled CDs making their way into the hands of powerful record company execs, or of Gwen Stefani picking a copy out of the gutter and falling in love with the music and with us because of it. I was shaking with anticipation, now that it was a sure thing.

Steph watched us load the equipment from her porch, leaning against the frame of the front door. I waved one final thank you toward her from the driver's seat of my car. Her face contorted, attempting to smile back, but instead she grimaced, already regretting the decision to let us take away her beloved gear. Elliot was giddy with excitement in the front seat. I threw the car into drive and we sped off.

"Dude, I can't believe she said yes," Elliot gushed from the front.

"She's cool as hell, I toldja."

"Yeah but that mixer is worth more than this car."

"Fuck you," I shot back. He was right, though. My car was a shit. "Least I have a car."

We called the other guys to tell them the good news.

The night was a go.

We planned to record at Elliot's place. Not only was the house secluded enough so that the neighbors wouldn't call the cops on us, but Elliot's mom, Janine, was cooler than any of us and we all knew it. She smoked a lot of pot, but she wasn't a burnout. It calmed her down, helped her relax. So, it never freaked anyone out when we'd show up at Elliot's house and it reeked of fresh smoke. None of us in the band got high, but it was comforting to know that we could if we wanted to. Janine would be able to stand the all-night rock-out. She might even pop into the room and jam with us for a bit, if she was up to it.

Derek, our surprisingly intense heartthrob of a lead singer, said they'd gotten the strings and a few pairs of sticks for me, but were heading back to the store because Jesse, our overly-pierced-yet-sensitive guitarist had forgotten to grab pics. I checked my watch and realized it was already nearing six o'clock. We only had about twenty minutes before the music store closed, so they'd have to get a move on and make sure that we had absolutely everything we needed before leaving again.

"What about food?" asked Jesse, yelling from the front seat of Derek's car. "We're probably gonna be at this shit all night. Elliot, you have any food at your place?"

"Not really," Elliot chimed in. "Maybe I can talk my mom into getting us a couple pizzas, but we may want munchies and sodas."

"I've still got like twenty bucks, so Elliot and I will grab snacks. You guys hit the store again and make sure you get everything this time. If we're missing even one cable, the whole thing is fucked." I sounded a bit more serious than I meant to.

"Oh and Mira might come by, too. I told her we were hanging out tonight," Derek said.

We all liked Derek's girlfriend Mira. She usually showed up when we practiced or wrote new songs, but if they were canoodling in the corner all night, which they were known to do, it would take us twice as long to get through all the tunes we wanted to lay down.

"Okay, but she can't distract us. We're gonna be working our asses off all night."

"Jesus Simon, calm down, will you? It's gonna be fun." Jesse was always complaining about the way we said things to each other. But he was right. I was too excited.

"I know, I know. I'm paranoid now because I have Steph Bergeron's equipment and the future of our sexual relationship sits in the trunk of my car." We all busted out in big, dumb laughter.

We called ourselves The Kicks, a name that someone had said out loud for some reason we couldn't remember, and we all immediately clung to. Truth be told, it was the first name we'd come up with that wasn't embarrassing. It sounded like a badass seventies punk band, but really had no more meaning than that. Some people thought we named ourselves after cool footwear, some thought we liked Route 66. We'd gone through names like Pizza Pants, Sniper School, and for about two hours, we were fully committed to ZZ Bottom. So, when somebody finally threw out The Kicks, we stuck with it and moved on.

Elliot and I pulled into the parking lot of a small grocery store, a frequent stop for us before a band practice at his place. The owners knew our faces well, and even though we spent a fortune on candy and sodas, they still seemed to glare at us every time we walked in. We assumed they hated all teenagers, so their looks of disdain never phased us.

"Should we try to get some beers?" I asked, half-joking.

"I don't want any beer."

"My brother will probably get us some, if we pay him for-"

Elliot snapped at me. "I want to hang out and play, man. I don't want to get drunk and sloppy, we'll ruin the whole thing."

"Okay man, shit. I was mostly kidding."

He didn't apologize, but put his hands in his pockets, hunched his shoulders, and walked into the store. Elliot was a tricky kid to figure out. At first, he came across as shy, timid, afraid of everything. But once you got through that shell, he was this funny, confident guy, a delight to be around. But there was a darkness to him that reared its ugly head every now and again. He'd yell at someone out of the blue or get so mad at video games that he'd break anything that was close to him. It often took me by surprise, like in that parking lot, but usually by the time I'd registered it, he'd already moved on and we were fine.

My phone vibrated in my pocket. I could tell it was my mother calling. Her calls somehow had a distinct, angry vibration. I stayed outside and flipped open my phone.

"Hey Ma."

"Where are you? I thought you were gonna clean up the garage before I got home."

"I have to do it tomorrow, I'm with the guys–"

"I can't even park my car in there, Simon. Goddamnit. You need to do it tonight."

"Ma, I'm stayin' up to Elliot's tonight. We're recording, remember? I told you."

She paused. "I don't like you staying overnight at that house."

I stopped, unsure of what to say. My mom had never worried about Elliot before.

I asked her why she was worried, assuring her that we'd only be playing music all night, totally behaving ourselves.

She sighed, defeated.

"It's fine," she managed. "Just be careful. And tomorrow, the garage. No excuses."

"I will, I will."

"You have everything you need for tonight?" She said, moving back into nurture-mode. Despite hating our music, my mom knew that playing together was better than doing just about anything else teenage boys could be doing with their friends.

I assured her that we were set, mere minutes away from perching ourselves in Janine's huge upstairs room and putting out the purest rock and roll anyone had ever heard. I hung up, flipping the phone closed with one hand, showing off for no one, then I went into the store to help Elliot pick out the snacks for the night. We left with bags full of sodas, candy bars and a few bags of chips. We were ready.

The sun was setting. It was nearing seven when we saw Derek's car coming down the winding dirt road to Elliot's house. We'd already unloaded Steph's gear and

Elliot was hard at work assembling the whole rig. He was our bassist and reluctant engineer, when we needed it. The complexity of guitar sounds, the underlying tones, the effects and timbre, were all Elliot's domain.

That was all gibberish to me. I was the drummer, I just hit things. Even Jesse was still figuring out how his own guitar worked. He followed Elliot's lead, enough to hammer out a few chords here and there. Shredding solos would have to wait.

Derek fell naturally into the lead singer position. He was always in a neatly pressed but untucked shirt from the expensive stores in the mall. His parents were rich, but he hated them and hated being associated with the wealthy crowd, so he never made us feel below him. He was a great guy to have around, not just to cover us when we didn't have cash, but because he didn't need us. He could hang with the cool kids if he wanted to, but he genuinely enjoyed being with us, so he was the center of the tight-knit group.

Jesse and Derek lugged their amps up the stairs and into the large room that Janine had let us rip apart and hollow out. It wasn't being used for anything now that she'd kicked Elliot's dad, Harold, out of the house. I had no idea what the room was used for before, but Elliot had jumped on the opportunity to turn the empty space into his hobby room, so he did. Janine seemed cool with the change.

The closet door near the hallway had a massive dent in it, the cheap wood had broken through on the outside. I assumed Elliot had done the damage while moving something in or out. It looked to be about his body size; he probably lost his balance and fell into the door, shoulder first. I laughed to myself, my mom and dad would kill me if I'd done damage like that to our house. I'd try to remember to give him shit about it later.

My drums were set up in the back corner, facing the center of the room and the window on the far wall. To my right was Jesse's amp, then Derek's mic, and by the door were Elliot's bass and Steph's precious mixer. It looked awesome. Professional, even. I couldn't shake the idea that this was "the night when the internationally famous band, *The Kicks,* recorded their first album." After everyone had gotten settled and tuned up, I found myself foolishly wondering, *will this truly be a night of legend?*

When we were finally ready to hit record, I asked, "Alright, what first?"

After a pause and brief debate, we landed on the obvious choice, *Newsflash.* It was aggressive, angry, a scathing dissection of modern popular music, which at the time was dominated by watered-down boy bands with nonsensical lyrics and shitty rappers acting hard. It was the perfect tune to start out with, while the sugar from the snacks was hitting us. We could save the ballad for our inevitable crash later.

Without wasting time with a warm-up or a run-through, Elliot hit the big red record button and we dove right in. Derek belted out the chorus, screaming "*We want it hard as we are! We want it how we feel it!*" It was an anthem only for us, but we wailed. Our necks were sore after the first take. We thought we were capturing the energy and the spontaneity of our youth. We were certain we could move onto the next tune.

When we played it back through Steph's equipment, it was a sloppy mess. The drums and bass were off for nearly half the song, Jesse's guitar was slightly out of tune, and Derek's vocals were barely understandable. Quickly humbled, we all laughed it off, realizing that we'd actually have to focus, maybe pull back the antics a bit.

"Let's save the headbanging for the live shows," Elliot said, twisting a few nobs, adjusting our levels. We settled in again, readying ourselves for another run at it.

The next take was much better. Having heard the shit that came from not caring, all of us brought our musical skill and technique to the heavy song. Jesse managed an improvised lick that transitioned us out of the silly-sounding verse and into the floor-stomping riff of the chorus. My muscles had warmed up, my timing was right on. I hit every drum head with precision, every rim shot was perfectly placed. Once we hit that last note, we froze, waiting for the final chord to cleanly ring out.

"Clear," Elliot shouted as he clicked the recorder off. He seemed happy with take two and smiled big as he rewound the tape to play it back.

We all huddled around, excited to hear the pure beauty and genius we knew we'd captured. W hen he played it back though, we heard only a low muffled sound from the speakers, like the music was playing down the street. Elliot, brow furrowed, checked the settings on the mixer.

"Shit, fucking input levels were down."

He turned back to us, sucking in air through his teeth. W e weren't so genius after all. W e all slunk back, a bit deflated.

Derek rubbed his neck, shaking his head and smiling. "Fuck dude, this is gonna be a long night."

After almost four hours of straight rockin', it was approaching one in the morning. W e'd managed to get acceptable takes for each song and we'd been able to punch in over the major flubs. Elliot would edit the tracks later and make them sound professional. W e'd thankfully worked our way back to feeling good about the album. We could get this right after all, but it would be harder than we thought. The night was already long, but we weren't about to stop.

Janine poked her head in and found us sitting among a mess of crushed soda cans, smiling big, while we played back the best take of our tune, *Plastic Man,* (every high school band is required to have a song with the word "plastic" in the title).

"You guys still going up here, huh?" she asked.

"Yeah, got three songs done. Wanna hear?" Elliot said, excited to share.

"Oh, I can hear," she joked. Janine had been downstairs the entire time, doing her best to keep her cool, I'd imagine. She had the stink of marijuana on her, which I assume was helping her remain calm with all the racket. "You need anything?"

"Nah, we're good," Elliot replied without looking up.

Pulled out of the haze of creation for a moment, Derek remembered something he'd wanted to ask. "Hey Janine, would you mind if Mira came by tonight? She wanted to see us in action." The question was a formality, he knew she'd be okay with it. Janine kept an open house for Elliot's friends. But she always appreciated him asking.

"Of course, honey. If she still wants to see your ugly faces this late."

"Yeah, she's getting off work soon, so she was gonna

stop off and hang out for a bit."

"Tell her I'll leave the front door open."

Janine left us then, and after a quick reset of the gear, I threw back the rest of my warm Coke and I sat down at the drums. We'd decided to move onto the next tune, *Celestialism*. I couldn't tell you what that one was about, even now. But it was heavy and difficult to play, so before we started, I used my drumsticks to twist my hands around, stretching out my forearms. We were only half done, so I had to stay loose.

As I sat there adjusting my throne, I watched the guys grab their guitars and level the mic stand. I found myself in a quiet moment of contentment. I was happy, but more than that, I could feel that this was the kind of thing I was meant to do. I was having an amazing time with my closest friends, laughing, messing around, playing our own music, and we would have something great to show for it. We were ready to play all night and get every one of our six original songs recorded.

We'd landed a couple decent takes of *Celestialism*, but knew we needed a couple more, maybe another swing at the guitar solo if we wanted to impress anyone. In the middle of the song, out of the corner of my eye, I saw movement through the window, gliding through the trees. I tried not to let the headlights distract me, but it had been dark for hours, so the light was a shock. I brushed it off and kept playing, thinking it was Mira. I attempted a drum fill that I'd never tried before and nailed it.

The song ended a couple minutes later and we all froze again, letting our last chord resonate in the thick air of the room. But as the sound of the music faded, we heard something unexpected. Voices. Loud. The band members exchanged a few glances, but we figured out pretty quick who it was. All our eyes fell on Elliot. He frowned, his shoulders hunched in that same posture I'd seen earlier. I watched all the hope and joy drain out of him with the realization of what was happening. He knew the extent of the situation before we did, so he was already embarrassed and apologetic while we were still confused.

"Is that your dad," I stupidly asked.

"Hold on, I'll be right back. Sorry guys," he mumbled back.

Elliot took the bass from his shoulder and leaned it carefully against the wall before walking out, closing the door softly behind him. Derek slipped the mic back onto the stand and plopped himself down on a chair, cracking open another soda. He'd been the only one drinking the ginger ale and had gotten through half the case. It was nearing two in the morning; our energy was waning.

"Break time, I guess," Jesse muttered, half annoyed,

half glad for the rest. Jesse and I put up our gear and lay down in the middle of the floor next to each other. I'd been sitting on the tiny throne for nearly six hours, pounding away on the drums and swinging my shoulders from side to side, so when I stretched out, my spine sang with a series of cracks and pops from my neck down to my butt. Jesse let out an old man groan as his knees were finally bent, his baggy jeans rustled against the dirty tan carpet.

Downstairs, the voices grew louder. Elliot had joined in, although his voice was far quieter than that of his parents. The three of us sat in the room a while, maybe twenty minutes; talking over whatever shit we'd forgotten about in the chaos of preparing for the night.

Shouting voices pounded their way through the walls, muffled and angry. We all jumped at a loud crack from downstairs. Something had hit the wall hard, now footsteps marched up the stairs toward our room. Jesse and I exchanged a look as we both shot up from the ground. We didn't want to be caught laying on the floor. The footsteps stomped their way to our floor and the door swung open.

Janine came in and slammed the door behind her. Her lower lip quivered, her eyes opened wide, her chest heaved up and down with deep, panicked breaths.

"I'm sorry boys. I don't want him here. Don't say anything to-"

The door was shoved open, forcing Janine into the room. Harold Voss, Elliot's father, stood there in the open door for a moment. His head wobbled on his neck, and when he steadied himself, he saw all the musical equipment we'd packed in there. The smell hit us all right away, that thick stinging stench of B.O. and beer, bad breath and cheap cologne. An unlit cigarette dangled from his lip. Harold was dead drunk.

"Wha's goin' on in here," he mumbled, trying to sound upset.

"We're recording tonight, I told you," Elliot all but whimpered from behind him.

"I din't- you din't say all this." Harold looked us over with contempt. "Well hiya boys!"

"Hey, Mister Voss," I said. Jesse half-heartedly waved. Derek stayed noticeably quiet on the couch, arms crossed over his chest.

Janine placed a gentle hand on Harold's forearm. "Okay, let's go back down-"

"Fuck off a' me, I'm talkin' to these boys." The cigarette fell from his lip to the floor. Harold didn't notice.

His hair was matted from sweating under his hat all night. His wiry frame swayed back and forth, trying to find that ever elusive balance, hidden by the booze. I'd met Harold once a few months back when I stopped by to pick up Elliot on our way to a movie across town. Harold was quiet then, nervous, kinda nerdy, but notably shy and reserved. This drunken buffoon was making an ass of himself. I was certain I'd never met him before.

My dad came home this drunk only once, and my mom and I made fun of him the entire time. I assumed this night would end up the same way, with everyone laughing about how silly it all was, but Elliot's face never changed from that pained, embarrassed frown. He knew what this was. I didn't. Not yet.

"I'm talkin' a my son's friends, Janine. In ma'own house."

"We should leave them be, Harold. They're working."

"S'two in the mornin', you mean to tell me I can't come home t'my wife and my son? I find these guys fuckin' rockin' out upstairs." Harold mimed a clumsy guitar, mocking us as best he could manage. "Can hear it from the end a'the fuckin' driveway. D'you ask me for p'mission? Hmm?"

Still not grasping the seriousness of the situation, I looked up and realized he was staring right at me. Spittle decorated his lower lip and his chin. His eyes were open wide, waiting for my answer. I let loose a smile and tried to be as nice as possible.

"Sorry Mr. Voss. We asked Elliot if we could use this room."

"You j'st asked Elliot. He's sixteen years old, you think this is his place?"

He stared at me for another intense moment. "You know what this room used to be? Hmm?"

I looked to Janine. Her eyes were down. I looked over to Elliot, but he had turned away. I shrugged, hunching my shoulders like Elliot always did and answered, "No idea."

"It was mah gun room."

We let that awkward bit of information hang in the air.

He continued, "It's where I kept my instruments fer killin'."

Janine bravely chimed in, "And now it's not a gun room. Your son plays music in here." She brought her eyes from the floor to meet his glazed-over look, and in that moment, my stomach tied itself into a cold knot. We all held our breath. I wondered what I'd do if he got angry, if he screamed at us, if he hit her. Thankfully, he just snorted and brushed it off.

"That's right. Now I got my guns in a tiny little closet in my apartment cross town. Now my gun room has a bunch a' rock an' roller kids blastin' at two in the fuckin' morning."

He scoffed at us with disgust and swung around and

left the room. Elliot followed him down the hallway toward the bathroom and tried to make sure his father didn't tumble face-first down the long staircase.

Janine cried, "I'm sorry guys. I'm sorry." She turned and left quickly.

"You don't have to apologize," Derek called out after her, but she was already gone.

Once Derek, Jesse and I were alone again, I snorted a quick, uncomfortable laugh. But once I saw Derek's stone-faced expression, I felt an instant pang of stupidity.

"He's so fucking drunk," I reasoned.

Derek wouldn't budge.

"It's not funny," he declared with a grimace. And suddenly, I understood. This was a bad situation, one that needed to be handled carefully, one that could quickly spiral into something far worse if we made a wrong move.

All I could manage was a dumb-sounding, "Oh."

Derek ripped a beat-up silver flip phone from his pocket and hit a few buttons. With the phone to his ear, he got up and started pacing, waiting for whoever it was to answer. Jesse and I exchanged a concerned look. "Are you calling the cops?" Jesse's voice quivered at the thought.

"No," Derek replied, biting his nails.

Another huge thud came from downstairs, followed by a crash of broken glass on the tile floor. I shot toward the door, opened it, and nearly tripped over one of the cables from Steph's mixer. From the top of the stairs, I caught a glimpse of Harold on the ground next to a toppled side-table and a shattered vase. Janine was on her hands and knees, doing her best to pick up the big pieces of glass while Elliot crouched behind his dad, doing his best to pull him up from under his shoulders. Harold's laughter was obnoxious.

"Fuck," Derek muttered at the sound of the voicemail. "Em, don't come to Elliot's tonight. Just go home and I'll talk to you in the morning, okay? … It's not a good night. Trust me, please." He hung up and sat down again, burying his face in his hands. I stepped back into the music room and eased the door closed.

"How bad is this?" I was mostly trying to fill the thick silence in the room.

Derek's sweaty, red-faced exasperated look was enough of an answer, "I was here when he did that." He pointed to the busted closet door I'd noticed on my way in earlier. "One second we were all laughing at something stupid, and the next, he shoved Elliot through the door."

Standing in that room, Elliot suddenly made a lot more sense to me. I suppose if there was a chance of my body getting slammed through a wooden door with a single wrong word, I'd keep quiet, too.

More shouting rumbled from downstairs. Harold

yelled something incoherent again. Muffled through the walls, he sounded like the Peanuts version of the devil. I heard more stomping, coming closer and closer to our room.

"Ah fuck," I said as I moved away from the door. Sure enough, Harold shoved the handle down and pushed it open hard enough to slam it into the wall.

"Play somethin'!" he shouted with disdain. "Let's hear some f'kin' music!"

None of us moved until Elliot came up the stairs behind him. "Dad, come on, stop," he pleaded.

"You want to play in my gun room, go on, let's hear it." Harold sat himself down hard on the wooden chair in the corner and made a show of waiting for us.

Elliot stepped into the room, eyes down, hands stuffed in his pockets. "We're not gonna play with you in here."

When none of us grabbed our instruments or made a move in their direction, Harold let loose an inhuman, guttural scream, "PLAAAAY!"

Elliot grabbed his bass, and muttered, "Let's just play something."

Following his lead, Derek clicked on the microphone and bit his lip. I slunk down behind the drums, shoulders hunched, head down. Jesse slung the guitar over his head, throwing on his baseball cap and pulled the visor down to hide his face. Elliot switched the mixer back on and strapped on his bass, wiping away tears he thought we didn't see.

"What's next," Elliot asked.

"Sumpthin' good," Harold said, then belched.

"How 'bout we try *Nonsense*," Derek threw out.

Elliot didn't wait for a reply from anyone before saying, "Cool, let's do it."

The song would be a temporary, though welcome distraction. If Harold sat for long enough, maybe he'd pass out, although I doubted a dead person could sleep through the song we were about to play. Nevertheless, Elliot hit the big red record button and turned to us, ready to go. Derek looked at me and nodded. I took a deep breath and counted us off.

The tune, *Nonsense*, was an angry song about the absurdity of leadership, how it's impossible to remain un-corrupted while being responsible for so many people. With clever lyrics like, '*You're moving under false pretense you make it sound like self-defense, when everyday you've done the same and run me out of my own name,*' it seemed relevant. We landed on every beat with a fat, heavy, distorted chord that hit like a truck. We played with everything we had.

Hammering through the loud song, all of us avoided the blood-shot eye contact with Harold. His chair creaked as he moved around to the music, bobbing his head toward the ground, his feet tapping to the beat.

A couple times, he pounded his fist into his leg and screamed, "Yeah! Yeah baby!" Like he was at an actual concert instead of his son's home-recording session. When he had the energy, he started headbanging hard, his greasy hair whipped around, throwing tiny drops of sweat across the room. He looked possessed by a demon hell bent on tearing his body apart from the inside. The song came to a climactic end with a shrieking high note from Jesse. That last note landed a bit sloppy, but Harold shot out of his seat, clapping over his head and shouting, effectively ruining the take.

"Yeah! Motherfuckin' rockin', hahaha!" We stood in place, unsure of what to do or say. Harold slammed his hands together in aggressive applause. "Y'all are pretty fuckin' good."

The recorder clicked off. Harold threw his arms up in exaggerated confusion. "Hey, I thought you were playin' a show! You gonna stop the show?"

Elliot had had enough. The night had soured and he was pissed.

"We're not playing anything else." Elliot said through a clenched jaw.

Janine snuck into the room then and stood quietly in the corner like a chaperone.

"What, you done? It hit two-thirty and you call it quits? Thought rock stars went at it all night." He turned to Janine. "How many songs they play for you, huh?"

Before she could say anything, Elliot spit back, "We played a song for you. Can you get the fuck out of here now?"

Elliot may as well have slapped him in the face.

Harold stood for a moment, deciding how to react. A little smirk crept onto the corner of his mouth. His eyes narrowed, he lunged forward and grabbed for Elliot's sweatshirt, but instead shoved him backward with a clumsy fist. Janine shot forward as Elliot stumbled and fell onto his back, the neck of his bass smacked my mounted toms and sent a hollow thud from the center of the room. Derek took a step toward Harold ready to fight; Jesse took a step back to the wall, and I shot up to my feet, not sure whether to dive after Harold or to help Elliot off the floor.

"You talk to your father like that?!" Harold shouted over Janine's shoulder.

He screamed a few nonsensical threats, spewing bullshit about what his own father would have done to him, while letting his wife stop him. Derek took a step toward them both, ready to defend Janine if he had to. She put her hand up and Derek paused, but stayed within arm's reach.

Harold continued his verbal assault while I tried to

help Elliot to his feet. "This is what happens when you live here alone with your mother. You're a fucking pussy," he said, for the first time speaking with perfect clarity.

"That's it," Derek said, turning away in disgust. He pulled the phone out of his pocket again and dialed.

"Derek, no," Janine pleaded. "Honey, don't do that. Please hang up."

Derek let out an exasperated sigh and flipped his phone closed which got Harold's attention.

"Whatchu doin'?"

"You don't calm down I'm calling the cops, man." Derek's anger was boiling over. The knot in my gut squeezed tighter and I realized it had been tightening since the moment Harold showed up. I could barely breathe.

I saw Janine's face drop with dread. Harold swatted her hands away and stepped toward Derek.

"The cops, now why would you do that? We're only talkin' here."

"I'm not your kid, Harold. I don't owe you shit. And you're being an asshole."

We were shaking. All of us. I couldn't believe the balls on Derek, but I remembered that his old man was no picnic either. He was used to dealing with something similar. My parents were both happy people, got along with most everybody and when they drank, they laughed a lot more. I trusted Derek more than myself in that moment.

Harold leaned in close to Derek's face. "You bring the cops here, I'll kill you."

Derek remained calm. In fact, having the threat unveiled and out there for all to hear made the situation clear. Later, I learned that Derek had a pen in his pocket and he was ready to shove it through Harold's eye. That's what kept him under control. I'm glad I didn't know that then.

"Stop it, both of you." Janine found her anger now, too. "Nobody is calling the cops, and nobody's fighting, understand?" She put her hand on Harold's bicep, pulling him away from Derek. "Now Harold, we interrupted their recording session. Let's go downstairs and you boys can pack up, okay?" Her eyes opened wide, like she was performing for the cheap seats. She was desperate for us to agree. She looked over at me and nodded with frantic affirmation.

"Yeah, I think we're done anyway," I spat out feeling like I needed to contribute to the de-escalation somehow. All it did was pull Harold's attention to me, but that was enough. He didn't want to bash *my* face in, at least not yet.

"Get out," Harold muttered to himself. Drunkenness took hold of his lips again, and he stepped toward the door like an angry 5-year-old after being scolded. The rest of us breathed a collective sigh of relief with him out of sight. Janine ducked out after him, tears flowing down her cheeks now. My heart melted for her in that moment.

I put a hand on Elliot's back as he sat on his amp, shoulders slumped, head down.

"You okay, man?"

Elliot sniffled and wiped his cheeks, "He's such an asshole."

"I didn't know it was that bad."

"My mom kicked him out like three months ago, but he still shows up sometimes. Usually after he drinks. Mostly he's just sad and he sits in the living room and cries, but sometimes..." He trailed off. We knew what he meant.

Derek walked over and knelt next to Elliot. "Fuck him. Let's wait until he passes out, pack up our shit, draw a dick on his face and go, okay?"

Elliot laughed and wiped his face again. "I should probably go help my mom."

Derek shook his head, "Sounds like she's got him handled. You should stay here, with us. Keep out of his eyeline, you know?"

"If we hear something, we'll run down there," Jesse said, coming back into the fold.

We packed up our gear, any happiness or sense of accomplishment evaporated and left us with only the weight of exhaustion from lack of sleep and the all-night jamming. Dried sweat had caked on top of my skin and I grew more uncomfortable by the second.

For about twenty minutes it was quiet and we'd all begun to shake the strangeness of the night. Elliot copied the last of the tapes he needed before he unplugged the cables to Steph's mixer, but as he bent over to set his legs to lift it, a new set of headlights shone through the trees and came up toward the house.

We all froze. Janine had been downstairs with Harold for a while, maybe she'd calmed him down enough to call a taxi for him. Maybe Harold had called whatever friends he'd been drinking with earlier to have them over for a rockin' good time. Maybe it was the police. Derek looked out the window in a panic when he saw the lilac Dodge Shadow pull up to the house.

"Fuck," he looked back at us, eyes wide.

Derek rushed for the door and I followed close behind. We were at the top of the stairs when we heard the knock on the front door. Harold was nearly passed out on the couch at that point, a half empty cup of coffee on the table next to him. But the light rapping on the door brought him right back up and he pulled himself off the couch, ready for another fight.

"W   ho the fuck? It's three in the damn morning," he muttered as he marched forward.

Derek reached the bottom of the stairs when the door

whipped open and tiny little Mira stood on the porch. She flashed an adorable, dimpled smile, acknowledging the lateness of the hour. "Hey, Mister Voss. The boys still here?"

Harold looked down at her feet. The bright, neon green sneakers grabbed his attention first, but his gaze moved up her smooth legs, to small denim shorts, perfectly cuffed high on her thighs. Her cleavage was small, though plainly visible beneath her tight undershirt. Her brown hair was tied up in a messy pony tail. At seventeen, Mira was pretty, well on her way to an absolute knockout. Harold stared at her, and from the other side of the large kitchen, I saw him shiver and straighten his back.

"It's Mary, right?" He said.

"Mira," she corrected with a polite smile.

"Right, Mira. Yeah, they still here. Havin' a bit of a party," he said, smoothing his hair.

"A party? Well that certainly sounds like something they'd get up to."

"Well come on in, hell. It's cold out there." Harold put a hand on Mira's bare back between her shoulder blades and escorted her inside. His mouth hung open as he looked down at her ass. It was perfectly round, highlighted by every graceful step she took. Harold swallowed hard.

Derek stood near the bottom of the staircase, looking panicked and afraid. I put a hand on his shoulder to remind him that I was there. He locked his eyes on Harold who looked up from gawking at Mira, his tongue pressed against his teeth, breathing loudly through his nose. He looked hungry, ravenous.

Mira didn't notice the worry in Derek's eyes, and met him at the stairs, lifting herself as she usually did on her tip toes to kiss his cheek.

"You didn't get my message?" Derek held her face in his hands, telling her the whole story with his wide eyes.

"Oh, I didn't check it," she said, hearing the slight quiver in his voice. I saw her face drop as she realized she'd walked into a terrible evening.

From behind her, Harold stumbled toward the fridge. "C'mon, let's go!"

"No honey, you need to come to bed, let these kids have the rest of their evening." Janine tried to bring him back to calm.

"Get the fucking beer out of the fridge, I know you got a twenty-four pack in there." He positioned himself between us and the front door.

"You know, it's pretty late," Mira attempted, valiantly. "Maybe we should go."

"Nonsense! Not 'fore one drink. C'mon, what other parents gonna let you drink a beer or two in their house, huh?"

Through Harold's veil of attempted charm and party guy attitude was something dark, demanding. His smile reminded me more of a snarl and I wondered how I'd ever be able to shake the image of this aggressive animal cornering us, preparing to strike. After no one replied for a few seconds, I tried to intervene, to ease the tension and keep us in the happy place, even if it was a mask on us all.

"Why don't we go back upstairs? I forgot my sticks. I need them tomorrow." Derek shot me a look like I was the chicken-shit in the group. I shrugged back at him. What else could we do? Fight him? No, at least not yet. Not unless we had to.

"There we go! Simon the fuckin' party animal!" Harold went to the fridge himself, probably forgetting that he'd asked Janine to do it, and pulled out the heavy case of Bud Light. Mira stood by Derek, clutching the back of his shirt while Harold lumbered toward them. Now, she understood.

At the top of the stairs, Elliot watched from afar. He walked back to the room first, head lowered even more than before. I turned to follow him, and Derek started up behind me. Mira was the last to head up the stairs, nervous about turning her back on Harold. At that point he smelled like a brewery that's been overtaken by black mold.

I looked back, Harold stood at the bottom of the

stairs, staring slack-jawed at Mira's ass again as she rose up to his eye-level. We all knew she looked good, of course, it was hard to deny that she looked hot in her skimpy post-work outfit, but Harold was practically in heat. Frozen in place by desire, Harold muttered to himself, "Jesus Christ, look at that." He was shaking his head in disbelief, the same way you'd marvel at a masterpiece in a Paris museum. Mira turned around at his voice and saw him staring. She pulled her shirt down over her shorts, but it was far too short, and she only managed to reveal more cleavage.

"Remember when you looked like that, Janine? Huh?" Harold had apparently abandoned any effort to conceal his thinking now. "Ha! Lost that tight little thing decades ago."

"That's enough," Janine fired back.

Derek had stopped on the top step and stood, staring down in disbelief. "You say one more thing about her, I'll come down there and break your fucking nose." He meant it. I could see in Derek's face that he wanted Harold to say something else, to earn a solid punch in the face to pay for what he'd already said.

But Harold barely noticed him. His eyes remained glued to Mira, to every bit of skin she was showing. His mouth hung open and he panted loudly. He took one step forward, within arm's reach of Mira. Derek waited on the stairs above her. Mira was stuck between the two of them.

"Whatchu think girl, you want to thank me in advance for those beers?"

I saw what was going to happen right before it did. Harold let the case of beer fall to the ground with a thud, then reached out and grabbed Mira's tiny arm above her elbow. She yelped in surprise as Harold pulled her back down the stairs, away from Derek. Gravity forced her to fall back into Harold's arms and he wrapped her up like captured prey.

Janine and Derek both leapt into action, but neither of them got there in time. Harold groped Mira's breasts. He grinded his crotch into her backside.

"You wanna fuck me?" he whispered through his teeth, drooling on her bare shoulder. He grunted with each thrust of his hips.

Mira tried to pull away and pushed against his arms, but Harold used all his strength to hold her in place. He shoved his hand up her shirt and rubbed his bulge against the back of her denim shorts, snarling like dog. Mira screamed.

Derek flew down the stairs with little regard for how he'd land. Janine worked to wrench Harold's hands away from Mira. Derek was all fury when he attacked Harold with several wild punches, most of them hitting the side of Harold's head or his arms, none with a significant effect. Harold barely felt the pain anyway. The hits probably hurt

Derek's hands more than anything else.

I started back down the stairs at the sound of the first fist. The smacking sounded like someone pounding meat.

Janine screamed, "No, stop! Stop hitting him!"

But Derek was no longer in control of himself.

There was already blood on Harold's face when I got down to them. I rushed to Mira, trying to pull Harold's boney hand from her arm, but his fingers dug deep into her flesh, turning her skin white. Tears streamed down her cheeks. The grip must have hurt. We locked eyes for a moment in the chaos; both of us wide-eyed and afraid. We pulled and twisted, and finally Harold's hand came loose. Mira fell forward and crawled out of the fight. I followed her.

With an open target, Derek landed a few strong punches to Harold's face. Janine pleaded for Derek to stop. Harold's face was beet red, blood from his lower lip smeared across his cheek, eyes filled with rage and the dullest sense of pain. He wasn't throwing punches, just reaching out to grab Derek, struggling with no real direction. He was like a wind-up toy let loose in a hamster wheel. He'd go where gravity moved him.

He got those bony fingers around Derek's lapel and his vice grip tightened. He pulled Derek in too close to throw any more punches. The two of them, mostly shoving each other around the kitchen in frustration, barreled through the wooden stools at the counter and knocked over two ceramic vases on the side table. They shattered, tinkling as they spread across the tile floor. With one strong heave, Harold shoved Derek backward. They both lost their footing and fell to the ground, rattling the dishes on the counter.

Harold worked his way on top of Derek, but instead of throwing punches, he held him on the floor, pushing his face and his shoulders down, as if trying to shove him through the floor and into the basement. Derek pushed back, but he was growing weak. He twisted his head around, red-faced, eyes bulging with effort, and looked at me.

"C-cops," he managed through a grimace. I nodded.

"No, please," Janine begged.

My phone was upstairs, sitting on my drums. But Harold heard clearly the word 'cops' and as if in slow motion, he turned to me. I locked eyes with him and for a single, tense moment and I thought I would cave, forget the phones and hunker down in the corner until this was all over. But I steeled myself and in one quick move, I let go of Mira and turned to charge up the stairs. Behind me, Harold launched himself toward me dropping Derek onto his back. I pushed passed Elliot and Jesse, who watched the whole fight from the top of the staircase. Harold all but ignored Mira now. He stomped on her hand as he crawled over her, growling.

I burst into the old gun room and for the first time

noticed the lingering smell of gun oil. After learning what the room was originally used for, I couldn't smell anything else. My phone sat on the floor tom, right where I'd left it. I moved toward the drums, but felt a hand grab the back of my t-shirt and pull. Harold had leapt over the last few steps and caught up with me. Off-balance, I lunged forward, trying to pull away. My t-shirt stretched, choking me a little as I was halted, short of my goal. Harold's grip was strong, and he used me for balance.

He pulled my face close to his and mumbled a string of incoherent threats. His stench was putrid, his hot breath thrown in my face with demands that I obey him, that this was his house, his room. The smell nearly crossed my eyes and knocked me out. I fell back and flailed my arms as I braced myself to fall against the side of my drum kit, knowing I would probably break either my gear or my bones. My right cheek hit the side of my crash cymbal, hard. The thin metal disc got its revenge on me after years of smashing it with a stick. My body spilled into the snare drum and rolled into my hi-hat, which was sent flying backward. It smashed onto the floor and tore a hole in the carpet.

Harold got it worse. As I fell, he lost his balance and tumbled backward toward the door. I looked up as the back of his shoulders plowed into the mixer. Steph's mixer. Elliot hadn't finished packing it up. The whole rig, set up on a flimsy drum case and empty boxes, came down in an expensive avalanche. Harold landed against the wall and hit his head with a sickening thump. The head and the mixer, both so new, so clean and beautiful, smashed onto the floor and exploded into pieces. All the knobs shot off, sending tiny bits of broken plastic everywhere. They were still plugged into the wall, so when the circuitry inside busted and snapped, a handful of blue sparks shot out from under the faders like tiny fireworks. Harold and I shielded our eyes.

There was a shower of dangerous, dancing electricity, a massive pop of red, like an exploding light bulb, then nothing but thick, acrid smoke as the mixer gave one final death cry. In that moment of relief at not being electrocuted, I felt my cheek growing hot, I touched it, feeling blood and stinging pain. I checked my hands and my arms for any broken bones. I'd lucked out with only a cut on my cheek and a handful of bruises on my limbs and my ribs. Nothing serious. Harold sat with his back against the wall, in a daze, his drunken eyes trying to make sense of what had happened.

Elliot charged into the room at the sound of the crash. His hands shot up to his head and he pulled his hair in frustration and despair. "What the fuck did you do?!" He screamed. Harold barely reacted. Elliot stepped over him and tried to look at the mixer. Everything Steph had loaned us was trashed. My heart sank to the floor.

I sat there staring at the mess, holding my bleeding cheek. Everyone had calmed down. Outside, I heard Mira's car start up and speed off down the driveway, presumably with Derek and Jesse in tow. It was just us. Janine marched up the stairs, yelling Harold's name. He was unresponsive. She barged into the room and saw the chaos he'd caused. She looked at me, saw my swelling cheek and at last, she didn't hold anything back.

"What have you done, you drunk sonofabitch?" Her lip quivered with shock and anger and for half a second, I wondered if we'd have to deal with a violent outburst from her, too. "Get the fuck out of my house! You piece of shit!" She was screeching now.

Harold was slow to get to his feet and he never lost the bewildered expression on his face as he walked out of the room and sauntered down the stairs. We heard his footsteps in the kitchen heading to the front door, calm and collected, his feet dragged and brushed through the broken ceramic on the tile.

Janine turned her attention to Elliot, on his hands and knees picking up pieces of the mixer. She bent down and put her arms around his shoulders, but Elliot shrugged off her embrace and stomped out of the room.

I saw the sadness wash over Janine and again, I felt pity for her as she wiped tears from her cheeks and looked to me. "Simon, are you okay, honey?"

I nodded, less concerned with my injuries than with the well-being of my friend and his mother. The engine in Harold's old truck kicked on and it rumbled slowly down the driveway. It was dangerous for him to be driving while drunk and with a possible concussion, but with him gone, the night could end in peace.

Janine helped me to my feet and together we walked downstairs. She apologized the whole way, shaking her head, rubbing my shoulders. I tried to tell her that I understood, that it wasn't her fault. I don't think she even heard me. She took me into the bathroom and cleaned the cut on my cheek, putting peroxide and gauze over the bloody mess.

Her tears were still flowing when I went out the door and walked to my car. I pulled the keys from my pocket, but before I slipped into the seat, the lamp in Elliot's room clicked on and I could see him there at his desk, facing his computer screen. He wasn't crying, didn't seem to be shaken any more. He was focused on something. After a few seconds, he slipped on headphones. I realized that Elliot was about to start editing the tracks we'd recorded. Knowing him, he'd be up all night, probably the rest of the weekend and by Monday we'd have a fully mixed CD to listen to.

I thought momentarily about going back in to offer my help in making the CD, but it didn't feel right. I assumed

Elliot wanted to be alone, to focus on something else. If I went up there, we'd end up talking about what had happened, making the whole event more real. If he didn't work on those tracks now, he might never go back to it. So, I got in my car, drove home and collapsed in my bed.

The next day, Elliot and I stood in Steph's living room, staring down at her rug while she screamed at us with tears in her eyes. I could see that she wanted to ask about my cheek when we walked in, but when she saw the remnants of the gear she'd lent us, she cared only about ripping us both a new one. As promised.

"W   hat the fuck happened? Did you run over it with a truck?"

Before I could answer, Elliot blurted out, "I dropped it down the stairs. I'm sorry."

I was taken aback at his answer. I didn't want to let Elliot fall on this sword, but if he didn't want to tell her what happened, I had to respect that. He promised to replace the busted equipment as soon as he could. He planned to give her all the money he made at his after-school job, he'd work over time to pay it off faster, swore that he'd help her with whatever she needed. Steph launched into a new wave of insults and angry reminders that now she wouldn't be able to record what she was supposed to record, and now she'd miss a couple auditions. Elliot and I nodded, taking our lashes as my romantic future with Steph, fictional or otherwise, evaporated.

In the car, driving back to my place to play some video games and relax, I tried to build up the courage to ask him why he lied, why he covered for his lunatic father. I thought I knew the answer, but I wanted to understand everything, for his sake and my own. As I opened my mouth to ask him, he pulled out a CD and shoved it into the player.

"Check this out," he said, as though we hadn't been screamed at a mere sixty seconds earlier. The music started, and I recognized it after the first note. It was our song Plastic Man.

"Holy shit, you finished this last night?"

"Only this one. Gotta do the rest this week."

I drove the rest of the way home with a big smile plastered on my face. The song sounded good. Really fucking good. I was proud, of myself and all the guys. Elliot had worked his magic, used some of our alt takes to fill in some blanks, correct all the errors. He'd done a great job on it, too. Everything sounded clear and professional. All mention of Harold ceased between Elliot and I. The CD had been a great distraction, and it was one we'd have forever.

He finished the CD, although it took him a couple of weeks to get everything to his liking. The band was through the roof about it. An actual recording of our music that had been, at least somewhat, produced. We played a couple more shows at our respective high schools, booked a show at a downtown event showcasing local artists, musicians, and food vendors, and at each of those performances, we sold copies of the five-song disc for two dollars each. We were thrilled when we brought home sixty bucks after the downtown gig.

We didn't talk about that night. Other than a few loaded "How are you's" with someone else who was there, nobody wanted to bring it up. But everyone seemed okay. Mira was the most shaken, but she never reported it to the police and we were pretty sure she never told anyone outside the group. I didn't tell my parents about the incident either, insisting that I'd hurt my cheek after some rough-housing with the boys. They were pissed, but they let it go quickly. I left it at that.

Elliot and I were the last two in town after graduation. My first semester in college started later than everyone else's and Elliot had decided to take a year off, to try and record for a few other local bands. Together, we had a great summer. The two of us were inseparable and when I eventually did leave for school, there was an Elliot-shaped hole in my life. I missed him instantly.

He never did go to school, having found a way to make some decent money on his own with recording and occasionally managing small-time bands around the state. I tried to keep up with him, but as it happens with old friends, we fell out of touch.

I wanted to shake off the whole town, let that dreadful night fade away into memory. And it did, for the most part. I went off to school in California and started playing with bands around LA. Most of them had some good shows, wrote a few good tunes, but ultimately fell apart.

I've recorded music plenty of times since that night, and even in the most stressful of situations, dealing with a demanding diva or an unpredictable coke-head, I've never felt the same kind of fear. A lot of that has to do with being an adult, but even so, no one has scared me as much as Harold Voss.

★★★

"Dad," Danny said and nudged my knee. "Is this yours or not?"

I snapped out of the daydream and stared at my son in a bit of a daze.

"Yeah, that was my high school band."

"The Kicks? Cool name." He gave an approving nod, which made me smile and brought me completely out of the melancholy.

I stood up from my desk and left behind the emails I was sending. They could wait. I dug an old disc drive out of a box full of junk and plugged it into my laptop, hoping it would still function. After importing the five tracks, I double-clicked the first one and cranked the speakers.

Danny listened intently, more into it than I thought he'd be. He tapped his toes to *Newsflash*, bobbed his head to *Plastic Man*, smiled the whole time *Celestialism* was on. While the familiar music played and I watched my son dance around, I told him about Elliot and the boys; all of us writing songs together, playing basketball when we needed a break, testing out my little brother's laser tag guns in the middle of the night, joking with each other about our girl troubles.

I didn't tell him that the same night we recorded those songs, Elliot's dad came home drunk and molested our pretty friend, or that he traded fists with our singer and threw me into the drum set, giving me the faint scar across my cheek. I didn't tell him that after that night, Derek had gotten fed up with our "trailer trash" lifestyle and stopped hanging out with us, altogether. I also didn't tell him that Harold Voss killed himself with one of his many guns after a similar night of drunken domestic violence, or that Elliot was currently in prison, serving a fifteen-year sentence for the rape of two underage girls, or that Janine died shortly after his arrest by taking too many sleeping pills and no one was really sure if it was an accident or suicide. I would remember those things forever, but I didn't want any of that darkness to take away from the happiness he was feeling from the music alone. Danny would have his own darkness someday. I didn't need to give him mine.

As the final chord rung out, Danny's big smile worked to wash away the awfulness of that night and help me find the joy in it again. Eyes big and ready to dance, Danny looked up at me and asked me to play them all again.

EVERYONE ELSE IS ASLEEP

Everyone else is asleep; everyone in my house, all the neighbors, certainly the rest of the people in town. I, of course, am wide awake. I should be asleep too, it's 2am. I'll probably fall asleep in school tomorrow. In the next room, I hear blissful snoring from my mother and father, but here I am, wide-eyed and fully conscious, tucked under the covers in my twin bed. Earlier, I dreamt I was an actor on stage for opening night, without a single line of the dialogue left in my head. That got my heart racing. Then I dreamt I was tasked with murdering my younger brother, whom I love and adore. That made my skin crawl, cold and damp. Lastly, I dreamt I was awake in my bed, trying to fall asleep. How ridiculous is that? Hard to remember where that one stopped and reality took hold; if it ever did.

Everyone else is asleep, and my nose is buried in a book. My mother has told me before not to stay up all night reading, but it slows my mind with focused thinking, conjuring only specific images built by carefully chosen words, blueprints of thoughts someone else once had. Nice to have something else projected into my head. The book is great, but terrifying. Full of ghosts, dragons, murders and bloody ends. I doubt I'll ever sleep again, wonder how I was ever brave enough to sleep at all.

The morning light ascends and brings no further rest. Still awake, though more tired with the sun finally showing itself, I put down the book and with no time for my usual shower, I throw on some dirty jeans and a wrinkled T-shirt and head down to the kitchen, where I'm supposed to meet the rest of my family for breakfast. I'm usually the first one awake, the first one in the kitchen, but today I'm dragging. I really hate the morning routine. Nothing bores me more than knowing exactly what's going to happen from minute to minute. My whole family is predictable, but they treat every day like everything that happens is so unexpected and exciting. It's nauseating.

But from the bottom of the staircase around the corner, I hear nothing but stillness. Not the usual frenetic energy of a makeshift breakfast, toast and coffee, or my parents yelling at each other because everyone's running late.

I step into the bright open kitchen and find my family doing what they always do. My mother stands by the fridge with the coffee pot in hand, my little brother Ricky sits at the counter, his forehead pressed against the marble countertop, as he does every morning while waiting for his cereal, and my father sits in his chair at the head of the glass table in the breakfast nook near the window, eyes buried in his tablet. But something is wrong; they're frozen in place like mannequins, as though they've been posed for an awkward family photo.

I rub my eyes; certain they're playing a trick on me. But when the stars clear from my vision, my family doesn't move so much as a hair. Statues carved from flesh. My mother holds a full pot of coffee above her laughably large mug, but her arms don't move and the dark coffee remains in the pot. The massive yellow mug sits empty. Her face remains stuck in a smile, in her usual morning cheer.

"Mom," I shout to no effect.

I rush over to Ricky and lift his head up, trying to get someone to talk to me. His eyes are fully open. For a split second, I'm sure he's dead as his head wobbles, his neck does nothing to stop it from slumping back. His face looks upward and reddens from being pressed against the countertop, there's still life in his eyes.

Only it's… stopped. Halted, somehow.

He's playing a game. They must be having fun with me, I think, but I know I'm wrong.

I place Ricky back where he was and check on my father next. Sitting frozen in his usual chair by the window, he has his e-reader open to the Washington Post, reading something that will surely upset him for the rest of the day. I check his pulse. It pounds away as usual. I take a step back. *This is a nightmare.* I run out of the kitchen, leaving the porcelain version of my family behind me.

Back in the comfort of my bedroom, I pack my things for school. I'll find someone there who can help, who can tell me what the hell is happening. Plus, Mrs. Goode will have my ass if I stroll in after the bell, no matter how strange the morning. My backpack is heavy with last night's homework, today's textbooks and an iPad I'm not supposed to bring. I walk out of the house, shouting, "Bye!" at my still-life family as I pass the kitchen. All I see is my mother's plastered smile. Her coffee pot is still full. *What else am I supposed to do?*

Outside brings me no comfort, no quick answers to the insanity of the morning. I hoped there would be someone there I could flag down and ask for help, someone else who could share in my confusion and awe. For only a moment, things look normal; joggers hog the sidewalks, a group of kids wait for the bus, irritated drivers stopped at the newly added stop sign at the intersection of Maple and Spring streets. Except, they're all frozen, all stuck in place. *So, it's not only my family.*

I walk over to my usual bus stop where a handful of my friends are arranged like a life-sized Norman Rockwell diorama. I rest a gentle hand on my friend Nathan's shoulder, afraid he'll break if I touch him too hard. He remains still, hunched over, mid-laugh, seconds after someone cracked a joke. Probably Wyatt, sitting on the curb next to him, a half-eaten PowerBar in his hand.

All these people stopped during their morning routines like someone hit the cosmic pause button on the most normal day in Old Orchard Beach. And the most pressing question bouncing around my skull; *why the hell am I still moving?*

An unexpected sound sails on the wind and startles me. A young man's voice. A familiar one. I whip around, to find its source.

"Corey!" Michael Obar's voice is a hushed exclamation. I search the street, my eyes landing only on statues and trees. Then, hidden behind Mr. Walden's bushes, Michael pokes his head out and waves me over. He's a couple of years younger than me, a sophomore; so, a senior like myself doesn't usually speak to a little piss-ant like him. Now, I'm happy to hear a voice, to see someone in motion. At least I'm not the only one running around out here. It's a strange sense of relief. It makes the world feel right again, but only for that instant.

I rush over to the bushes to Michael, who is still in his pajamas, faded images of the 90s Batman logo printed all over his legs. His loose-fitting white t-shirt is torn and tattered, his face scraped by the thorns and branches from his hiding place.

"Michael, what's going on?" My voice shakes.

"Quiet," His eyes dart back and forth, watching for any sign of movement on the street. That whisper yell is clearly going to be the tone of this conversation. He continues, "Everyone is asleep. I've been up for hours, but I haven't seen anyone else awake like us."

I take the same precaution and my head swivels left to right and back again. I see mannequins, statues, wax sculptures. Corpses? No, not corpses, but certainly not people.

"W hat you mean they're asleep? They look awake to me, just stuck."

"No, they don't have a clue what's happening to them," he sounds angry at my obtuseness, "but we can see what's going on. We are awake now, do you understand?"

I didn't, but I nodded anyway. "I don't know what to do," I say with a heavy glaze of desperation. The street remains silent and still, but I feel tension building.

Michael is terrified, and I don't think it's from the situation alone. "You just gotta act normal. Keep your head down, go to school, whatever you'd be doing right now."

"Act normal? How do I act normal right now?"

"Look at everyone, Corey. Think about it. What are they all doing?"

I take another look around, knowing what I'm going to see around me. The bus stop kids, the joggers mid-stride, they're all still there. "Nothing man, they're going about their fucking day."

"Exactly," he spits back. "That's exactly right. I don't know what you were up to last night, but I was out drinking with friends. I woke up hungover this morning to find this shit and I was late for the bus."

I think about my night. All I did was read. But I'm always reading.

"We're off the fucking tracks, man. Everyone else is in their usual place at their usual time, and they're all stuck like that. But we did something different, we screwed it all up."

All I can do is stare, slack-jawed and dumbfounded.

"What threw you off this morning?" He pleads for

confirmation of his theory.

I can only shrug my shoulders. It's easier than explaining my life to him.

Michael shakes his head, angry at my refusal to engage in his bizarre idea. "Well you need to figure it out. I'm gonna go out to the bus stop, just act normal. I think that's where I'd be."

Michael is much braver than I am. Me, I'm floating on a paper raft in a sea of childish fear and confusion.

"Okay, you coming with me?" Michael asks.

I shake my head. "I don't understand what you're doing, man."

"Just do what you do, I don't think they can find you."

My brow furrows. That's the first time I've heard about 'they'. *Who the hell are 'they'? Do 'they' know what's going on with my parents? Maybe I need to ask 'they' a few questions.* Michael sees the confusion on my face.

"You haven't seen them," his words a blend of sadness and caution.

"Seen who?"

Right on cue, a loud rustle spills from beyond the house behind Michael, followed by a guttural bellow, like an old man groaning through a thick, phlegmy cold. It's an animal sound I've never heard before. Something behind the house is alive.

"Trust me, steer clear," Michael says. "I'm going!"

He shoots up and runs away from the house, toward the bus stop. His footsteps are gunshots in the quiet of the street. The sound scares me into hiding. Whoever, whatever he's hiding from, I don't want "them" to catch me with him. I dive into the same place Michael hid for lord knows how long. I call myself a pussy as I watch Michael from the bushes. He runs down the street, stops near the group of statue kids at the bus stop, and freezes in place. Only it's not enough. I can hear his wheezing from down the street. If he thinks he's blending in, he's sorely mistaken. I'm nervous for him.

The rustling becomes louder and something big moves toward the street. I dive deeper into the bushes. The scratches and scrapes on my face match Michael's. I look over toward the house just in time to see it. A massive, hulking creature, at least twenty feet tall, steps out from the back yard and moves toward the street. My jaw drops. Loose leaves and dirt fall into my mouth and onto my tongue, but I dare not make the noise necessary to spit them out.

I'm surprised I couldn't see this thing standing behind the house. It's a mountain of a monster. The creature's tiny head, covered in thick brown leathery skin, sits atop wide, round shoulders. Its body is hidden beneath an acre-long, dirty shawl, but I get the impression of arms and legs beneath it. It walks slowly, deliberately, like a Jim Henson puppet, and when it turns to search the street, it reveals a hideous beak in place of a jaw. The yellow bone is cracked and stained with dark red splotches. It can only be blood.

I must be dreaming. Yet here I am, hiding under a thick bush, staring at this monstrous bird-thing in the center of a town filled with people frozen in place. My breath halts, remembering the dead quiet on the street. I see Michael's head turn, looking back toward this hideous thing. It swings its massive legs onto Spring Street and in that moment, I realize that it's searching for Michael. Either his footsteps or his panicked, heaving breaths drew its attention and now it marches toward the bus stop, clacking its broken beak in anticipation of a new meal.

Sensing the nervous trembling in Michael's limbs, the bird turns its head toward the group of teens. Looking on from my spot in the bushes, Michael looks like he doesn't belong. Not only is he still wearing his Batman pajamas, but he's chosen a stance that looks out of place. His back is against the front of the school bus. If things were moving along as usual, the bus would be in motion in the next few seconds. Nobody would be leaning calm and cool near the front grill of a school bus picking up kids. And if I can see how strange it looks from my obstructed view, I can't imagine what this nightmare creature sees with its eagle, or owl, or hawk, eyes.

It moves further down the street, each monstrous step

sends vibrations through the ground. Michael stops breathing when he sees the giant move toward him. With one final moment for action, he decides he's fooled no one and tries to make a run for it. He only gets a couple of good steps in before the bird-thing reaches out a shockingly long arm and snatches Michael off the ground, his feet left kicking and running in the air. The arm swings like a crane, bringing Michael closer and closer to its beak. Michael screeches an involuntary high-pitched sound and cries out as the bird-thing opens its beak and clamps it down on Michael's left arm and shoulder.

The edges of that broken beak must be sharper than they look, because with a single quick bite and swipe of its hand, Michael's entire left side splits open, and an ungodly amount of blood splatters loudly onto the pavement. Michael's cries stop. The bird-thing throws its head up, swallowing the piece of my schoolmate. I see it's thin neck bulging out as the meat descends down its throat toward its stomach. I assume it has a stomach. There's no telling what's beneath that acre of shawl, but I'd rather not find out.

Michael continues to drip as the bird-thing leans in for another bite, this time it's the entire top half, ribs to head. With a sickening wet squish, the blood and chunks of loose flesh pour over the busted beak like biting into a soaked sponge. I see how the bright yellow bone transitioned to the muddy, mustard-brown it is now. I close my eyes while the creature finishes off Michael's legs, slurping down the last bits.

Dreaming. I must be dreaming.

My body is cold, vibrating with terror. I try to calm my thoughts by counting down from ten, but I can't make it to five before my mind screams *Holy fuck, holy fuck!* It's all panic and fear, survival instincts. But those survival instincts betrayed Michael completely, so I can't make a move without a clear thought process, smart decision-making.

I open my eyes to find the bird-thing moving on, toward the nearby woods, away from me and my savior bush. It hasn't noticed me here. The only thing I can think to do is run home. I crawl out of the bush, careful not to rustle the branches too much, scraping my face more in the process.

I check the street to be sure that the coast is clear one last time and run. I keep my footfalls on the grass to avoid the echoing clap of rubber soles on concrete. I make it to my front door and I push it open, step inside, close it quietly behind me. The deadbolt slips into place as I carefully turn it closed. Won't do much good if the bird-thing decides it wants in, but it feels helpful.

A quick investigation into the kitchen finds my family still frozen in place, the coffee pot still completely full. I run up to my room to hide so I can think. My book remains on the nightstand where I left it. Part of me wants to grab it and dive in again, to lose myself in another world, in another mind, until somebody comes for me. But who knows how long it would take for me to be discovered? If ever. I sit on the floor, my back leaning against my mattress, and I close my eyes, concentrating.

Everyone else is asleep. That's what Michael said. I forget about the how, it doesn't seem relevant. Instead, I consider the why, the when. Everyone was in the middle of their usual routine. Everyone except for me. Except for Michael. He'd mentioned having a difficult morning. He was hungover. I was up all night reading, and I'd rolled out of bed far later than usual. I glance at the clock. 7:32am.

I'm late for school, I think to myself, letting out a single, snorting laugh.

But the idea sticks in my mind. This whole thing must have happened right as I walked downstairs at 7:32am. I'm always out by 7:20am at the latest. It's a short walk to school, but I know that if I don't leave the house by then, I'll miss the opening bell and I'll get hit with a tardy on my record. But I was still in bed that time. I wasn't where I'd usually be at 7:32am, when this whole thing happened, when everyone froze. Can it be that simple? That I didn't fall into the daily routine and therefore threw a wrench in the greater cosmic plan?

It seems absurd, but considering what gave Michael

away, his awkward position leaning against that school bus, it fit the strangeness of the situation. I do hate the daily routine of most people. My father relies heavily on the repetition for his work as a factory manager, my mother leans on it to retain sanity in raising two boys, but machine-like repetition unsettles me. I don't like school, I don't like the idea of college, and I despise the idea of deciding now what I'll be doing with my life in forty years. That's crazy to me. That's what I consider to be absurd.

But if that's the case, if that's what I'm fighting here, is my reluctance to fall in line worth dying for? Am I willing to be eaten alive, gobbled up by some radioactive Godzilla-bird to maintain absolute freedom? I resent being placed in this position, and a few drops of anger are added to my potent mixture of terror and confusion. Even if I'm not willing to submit, to conform, what can I do now? I've already gone off the beaten path and kept myself awake. I've seen behind the chaotic curtain.

My desk lamp rattles with the nearing footsteps of the creature. I panic for a moment, sure that it's come to find me and chew me up into mush. Outside my second-floor window, I see the bird-thing's face as it swoops by, moving with no purpose, at least not on the hunt as it was before. I check the clock again. 7:32am. When time stopped running or ceased to exist. I think back to where I was at that time.

That real time, anyway. I was still in bed reading about things not nearly as horrible as what I'm experiencing now.

I try to find where I went wrong. I can't imagine a reality where sleeping in is enough of a slight on the world to warrant a death sentence. But if that is where I strayed, and I wasn't supposed to be there at that moment, then where should I have been? The shower? On my way to school? I don't usually catch the bus, maybe walking along the sidewalk?

"Routine," I remind myself. All I can think to do is to follow the plan, start my morning from the first moment of waking and follow the daily pattern that annoys me so fucking much. Maybe that would help me figure something out, jostle some helpful thoughts loose. My hopes are raised at the thought that the world might be waiting for me, that my daily loop was the only one off the tracks, and once it's reset, we'll go on with our lives.

The vibrations in the floor return. The ceiling fan rattles. I crawl into bed and lay still for a few seconds. I close my eyes, mimicking sleep and try to behave like this were any normal morning, I pull down the covers and set my feet down on the carpet, remembering to fake a yawn and rub my eyes. I push open the door, letting the handle hit the far wall to let my mother know that I'm out of bed without shouting down to her.

I walk over to the bathroom, keeping my steps on the runner and off the cold hardwood floor. I click on the light and the fan and brush my teeth. First the top, then the bottom. Same order as always. The running water is loud, but I continue with the normal morning, washing my hands, my face, I'm not sure if it's a bad idea to bring attention to myself with all the noise. I step out and head down to the kitchen, where I know my family is waiting for me. The floor shakes, with heavier footsteps approaching from outside. I force myself to ignore them.

As I descend the staircase, feigning another exhausted yawn, the windows darken, shadows pass over them as the massive creature stands outside. It's come for me, I know it. But I don't waver. Nor do I look at the tree trunk-sized legs outside the living room window.

The bird-thing bends over, craning its head down to peer inside the window. My guts churn as that hideous face appears in front of me. My feet touch the first floor and I realize how big this fucking creature is. It could have swallowed Michael in one bite. And here I am, face-to-face with it. But I won't lift my head to look it in the eye. It wasn't in my morning routine.

I turn left into the foyer and move at my normal pace into the kitchen, finding my family right where I expected them to be. Where I always expect them at this time of day.

I look up at the crazy-faced smile on my mom's face.

"Morning," I routinely mutter to deaf ears. I'm already used to the silent reaction from all of them.

The whole room shakes as Broken Beak moves to the other side of the house, tracking my movements. The coffee spills from the pot onto the countertop. It ripples and sways with each massive footfall. I look around at my family one more time, this could be the last I lay my eyes on them. If I'm to be chewed up and swallowed by this awful thing, I'd like to have one final image of my family. And as final images go, this one isn't all that bad.

My mother smiles, my little brother adorably sleeps at the counter, my father, content in his chair. The only thing missing from this beautiful snapshot of everyday American life is me. The rebellious teenager. My seat at the breakfast table is empty. The chair is pulled out, my phone rests next to a plate of food laid out for me. Of course, my phone is there, I usually plug in my headphones and tune out my family during breakfast. That's the best part of my morning rituals.

Broken Beak leans its head down again and looks in through the huge kitchen window, seeing the family all together. It locks its eyes on me, clacking its beak together in anticipation of another fresh meal. Before it reaches in with its long slender arms and pulls me out of the house, I move toward my seat. It hesitates, and something flashes across its eyes. It looks like confusion. It tries to figure out why I'm not scared, why I'm not running.

When I sit, I rest my feet on the cross bar under the wooden chair, my normal position at the table. My legs go completely numb and suddenly, I can't move anything below my hips. They're totally frozen. I straighten my back and I feel it stick, like each vertebra is clicking into its proper place.

Outside, the bird-thing watches, curious. I calm down, pretty sure that the risk of being eaten is dropping with each passing moment (if the moments are in fact, passing), and I think I know what's happening to me.

I look down at my plate and reach for a slice of the bacon, cooked perfectly. As my fingers snatch the first piece, my whole arm freezes in place. Only my left arm and my head remain movable.

I look down at my headphones, I need to put them in my ears. Left-handed, it's a bit awkward, but I put the first one in. I can already feel my mind drifting away, like I'm waking up from a dream. The walls swim like heat waves. The plates in the cabinet rattle. This feels right.

As I move the second earbud to my ear, I turn my head and look Broken Beak directly in the eyes. It reacts with shock and pulls its head back in surprise. Its guttural groan shakes the glass of the window. I glare at it for a moment, my nostrils flare. With the creature's attention, I mustered all the strength I can and grumble, "I'll see you again, motherfucker."

Broken Beak makes a sound like a dying seagull and pulls its arm and attached claw out from beneath the shawl. I pop the earbud into my ear and click play on the first song that was up on the phone. A metal song. How fitting for the moment. And like that, with everything in place, I leave behind this horrific scene, the surreal Polaroid of my life, and just as the bird's claw crashes into the glass, everything dips to black.

★★★

SMASH! The window next to the breakfast table splinters and a black bird falls dead on the ground outside. Everybody jumps. My dad's head snaps up and away from his tablet, my mother spills her coffee everywhere and Ricky spins around in his seat, eye wide in surprise.

I rip the earbuds out of my ears and shout, "What the fuck was that?"

"Hey, watch your mouth around the kid," my dad says and stands to look out the window.

"Son of a bitch," my mom scolds herself, and sets down coffee pot, grabbing a rag. Coffee is everywhere. She does her best to clean it but moves fast across the countertop.

My father all but ignores the coffee mess and walks over

to the spider-webbed window to see the extent of the damage.

"Never seen a bird hit that hard. Christ, I'll need to get that fixed before it shatters everywhere."

"Scared the hell out of me," I say, still catching my breath.

My dad laughs. "Caught ya in a real daze there. Why are you so spacey this morning?"

"Just tired," I rub my eyes, trying to remember what I was daydreaming about. I remember a few flashes, images of awful things. Something about a stone wall with chipped yellow paint, stained with old red splashes.

"What were you doing all night," he asks, suspicious of wrong-doing.

"Just reading, Dad, relax."

"Reading all night, as usual," he mutters disapprovingly. But as he sits and goes back to his depressing newspaper, he does a quick double-take and looks closely at me. He pulls his glasses off and leans in, studying something.

"What is it?" I wonder, starting to feel a bit worried.

"What the hell happened to your face?"

I reach up and feel small scratches on my cheeks and up near my eyes. When I feel a stinging pain on my skin, I pull up my front-facing camera and look at the tiny cuts. I have no idea what they're doing there. I'm suddenly short of breath and I look out the kitchen window, half-expecting to see something there.

"Hmh, you used to do that to yourself in your sleep all the time."

That grabs my attention, "I did, seriously?"

"Yeah, you'd cry all night, then you'd be tired in the morning, mumbling about Big Bird."

"Big Bird?" I confirm. My spine rattles with a chill, giving me a kind of warning.

"I think that's who you were talking about. The Sesame Street thing."

I don't respond again. I let the image of Big Bird sink into my mind, but it doesn't seem right. It's the wrong color, the wrong voice. But the words, "big bird" are more accurate than he thinks.

"Guess it only makes sense," my father continues, "you never fell into a sleep routine then, why the hell would you now?" He sounds like he's given up on me.

My mother finishes wiping up the spilled coffee and glances at the clock.

"Shit, you need to get to school, Corey."

I'm not sure what it is, but a sharp pain shoots up to the back of my eyes and I gasp at the horrible idea of going to school.

"Can I stay home," I plead.

"What? Why," She said, perplexed.

"I just… don't wanna go today." I search for a good reason to convince her, but ultimately land on…

"It doesn't feel like I should."

Her reply is more confused than stern. "Well, I'm sorry you don't feel like it today, but it's a weekday, you're seventeen, that's what teenagers do. They go to school. So that's what you're doing, too."

I do my best to resist for a few more minutes, but when my father gets angry and lends his booming voice to my mother's side of the argument, I concede. Admittedly, I don't have much of a case to make. My father calls me rebellious, my mother says I'm creative, and my little brother thinks I'm funny.

But no one else sees what I see.

I go through my days watching everyone plod along through every hour that passes, with no idea what rests in the world beneath them. I watch them walk past and I can't help but think they're all frozen, they're all asleep, and I'm the only one with my eyes open, seeing the world for what it is. A consensual meat grinder.

For now, I go about my daily tasks. I take the bus to school, learn what the teachers teach, obey my parents as much as any seventeen-year-old does. And in the back of my mind, I do what I can to figure out what's causing this shifting feeling in my stomach.

It could be the idea that I'll grow old and die in this tiny little town, it could be the fact that my classmate Michael Obar disappeared without a trace (police suspect kidnapping and murder), it could be that I want to tear things down and watch society crumble.

But sometimes in the middle of the night, when I'm supposed to be asleep, I see a shadow pass by my window. Something big, ugly, and angry circles the house. I can't seem to shake the feeling that it's waiting for one of us to veer from the herd.

And so, I ask myself, *what if we all veered at once? What if we brought it all down together? What would we see? How much freedom would we find? And how many of us will it take to kill that big fucking bird?*

For full color prints of these illustrations and more, visit:
www.slomotionart.com

ABOUT THE AUTHOR

Billy Hanson is a writer and filmmaker, with projects ranging from music videos and comics to web series and films, including the acclaimed adaptation of Stephen King's *Survivor Type*, lauded as "one of the most jaw-dropping adaptations of (King's) ever made..." He has also written for the horror anthology comic, *Grimm Tales of Terror*.

Born and raised in Maine, Billy now lives in Los Angeles with his wife and son.